*All it takes to change the world are two simple things:
One extraordinary event and one incredible person.
So easy, right...*

A Brief History of Earth, humankind, and its demise. (If you needed a reminder...)

"The human race will ultimately be responsible for its own demise. It is with great certainty that I alert you of this now, and you heed my warnings. What we have called the 'benefits culture' hundreds of years has caused profound chaos to our world and its economy, and it is damage I fear we will not return from."
President of the USA, Harold Chant, the year 2465.

~~~~~~~~

"We need to find alternative fuels and a cure for overpopulation. But short of a miracle or genocide, I fear it's too late..." Queen Anastasia of England, the year 2989.

~~~~~~~~

In the year 3030 an alien species known as the Thrakorian's attacked Earth. On Invasion Day, the extraterrestrial race invaded the planet by force, however such influence was not needed. The Thrakorian's took control easily from the indigenous race that foolishly believed they possessed it, and any who opposed the new reign were killed instantly. Many were slain publicly to demonstrate that the invaders weren't interested in taking prisoners and some lives were taken just show how uninterested the Thrakorian's were in negotiation with the leaders of the old world. Soldiers stormed the streets, homes, businesses, schools and churches. They obliterated over half of all the human population on their first wave, and then enslaved the rest who would go on to either work or die under their new leader, King Kronus. They had travelled millions of light-year's to Earth for the invasion and the mission was carried out with precision and tact. It was by all accounts an easy harvest and the humans were left ashamed by their lack of fight—and rightly so.

Thraks looked human, and spoke their various languages, but soon replaced the previously adopted concepts of both nationality and race with a simplified version. Those who survived were given one language to speak exclusively—English, and were henceforth simply called 'humans.'

Their lives as they once knew were shattered by the new powerful regime. In the days that followed, humans were split into classes and sectors, microchipped like cattle, and put to work. None could match the strength, skill and intellect of the Thrakorian race, and their technology far surpassed that which the humans had once believed to be innovative and impressive.

From that day forward, every human knew their place and they would learn to be grateful for all their powerful masters had given them, or else suffer. The foolish, lazy, burdens on society previously used to getting a free meal and a roof given to them died in the streets, while their hardworking neighbors were rewarded with food and shelter. Only those who worked for their amenities thrived and the benefits culture was no more. Credits replaced currency and the only way to get them, was to earn them.

Nothing was the same again and their leaders enjoyed the order of things in their newly created world. Slaves were aplenty and there was much work to be done, so every human had a role to play. They either did it willingly, or died defying their powerful masters.

King Kronus had never once doubted the success of his mission, and quickly took his place on high for all to adore and worship, or else refuse and perish.

Rebels rose up to challenge his reign, and most were eliminated with no effort at all, but some remained. There would always be those who fought the regime, but the Thrakorian's loved a good hunt, so didn't mind one little bit.

And yet, there were huge discrepancies the likes of which most humans didn't care to see. But *she* saw them. Kyra Millan, probably the most devoted human soldier in Kronus's cause, but also the one with the most amount of questions. Despite everything she'd done and the ladders she'd climbed, or the friends in high places she'd made along the way, she saw through the lies. Kyra believed in him, and had told him so, but Kronus responded by calling her a fool. He'd made her life's work seem like nothing more than a waste of her time and talents, and then he'd sent her away without another word of explanation.

But, Kyra knew she would continue to serve him, for what else did she have without her unwavering loyalty to Kronus and his reign? She knew she had to find a way to balance what she knew and how she felt, however neither he nor any others of his kind were making it easy on her. Kyra's heart was breaking at being dismissed so callously, but she still yearned for his approval and cherished her place within his regime, so much so she's determined to fight him on the issue— even if she has to break every rule in the book in order to prove herself right.

Glossary of terms, and general information regarding the Thrakorian reign.
Earth's new class structure (in descending order):

King Kronus

Kings Guard Service (a separate entity to the regular Thrakorian army consisting of its highest honored members.)

Thrakorian Royal Armed Forces

Thrakorian civilians

Mixed-breeds (those whose families were forged years before Invasion Day to establish a presence on Earth prior to the arrival of their species. Many ensured they were appointed heads of state, or elected Kings and Queens of countries due to be overruled by King Kronus on his arrival.)

Gentry (Humans with extraordinary talent, intellect or skill worthy of a higher standing above all others of their race. They are handpicked by the King's chief advisors, and are expected to work hard if they want to keep their place. Many were branded as traitors to their race, while most were envied for the strength of will and readiness to serve—and their sinister tactics were well rewarded.)

Human Royal Armed Forces (dependent on rank)

Human upper-class

Human middle-class

Human lower-class

Convicts (those tried and judged by the Lawbringer for crimes against their King. They are treated like vermin, and ordered to work for nothing but basic food and shelter rations in service to their overlords, and housed in specialized areas away from the general human population. In return for training and further provisions, many well-behaved convicts are often given more responsibility if they show willingness and repentance for their crimes.)

Rebels (the lowest of all humans, and considered to be of zero worth to the Thrakorian reign. They are hunted down and killed on sight, while their sympathizers are gunned down or exiled in the arid lands formerly known as South America, where the radioactive atmosphere and barren landscape offered nothing but a long and painful death.)

<u>Human Royal Armed Forces rank structure</u>
(in descending order):

Gentry Officers:
    General
Elite Officers:
    Colonel
    Captain
Secondary Soldiers:
    Lieutenant
    Sergeant
Primary Soldiers:
    Corporal
    Recruit
    Convict

Thrakorian Royal Armed Forces rank structure (in descending order):

King Kronus
Kings Guard Service:
(Only one of each title is awarded, and they are master's of all soldier's beneath them.)

Chief of Defense
Lawbringer (judge and juror of all who stray from the laws)
Besieger (Capturer of rebels and rogues)
Master Protector (the personal guard of the King)
Marshals of the Army, Navy and Air force

Regular Thrakorian Royal Armed Forces:

Palodin (the highest rank bestowed on a soldier, given to those renowned for braveness, intellect, heroism and loyalty to the King.)

Lorde (a superior warrior, respected and heralded for their mastery in their field or fields.)

Duke (the strongest fighters and most experienced conqueror's.)

Sentinel (a soldier who guards their division and keeps watch over their comrades.)

Inquisitor (a soldier who's highly trained to seek out information, by any means necessary. Nothing is forbidden, and a long and painful death would come for any human who refuses them.)

Master (regular soldiers who work alongside humans to ensure they are following orders and not deviating from their given class and sector.)

CHAPTER ONE

Kyra was shaking with rage. She stormed out of the large meeting room and headed down the hall to the bathroom before Thrayke or any of the others could so much as ask what'd just happened between her and King Kronus. She failed to understand it herself, so didn't know where to begin to explain and she also couldn't fathom his reasons for having dismissed her the way he had. After all, it wasn't like she'd tried anything on with him, or ever brought attention to their history from Invasion Day, and yet he'd seemed downright angry with her for daring to show her face in his life again.

None of it added up. Kyra had served his cause almost her entire life and he'd called her foolish, silly, and idiotic for doing so. When she'd told him how loyal she was to him and his reign, Kronus had shot her down, when he ought to have been thanking her and every other human out there fighting to keep his world turning, while he sat back and did seemingly nothing atop a throne he appeared loathed to possess.

She'd dreamed of Kronus ever since he'd come to her aid that fateful day when his race had invaded Earth and had expected to find a powerful and driven King atop his human empire if she'd ever been graced with an audience again. Kyra knew now that she'd been so very wrong about him. Instead of being the authoritative Thrak she'd expected, he'd turned up in jeans and sneakers, and had seemed bored rather than impressed at hers and Thrayke's findings about the rebel gatherings. Kronus had a serious chip on his shoulder, about what, Kyra couldn't be sure, and as it currently stood, she didn't care to find out. His behavior was so ludicrous it was almost funny, but she certainly wasn't ready to laugh about it yet. If anything, she was still raging, and felt like she might lash out at the arrogant ass if he ever came near her again.

When Kyra finally left the bathroom, she wasn't surprised to find Thrayke—both her boyfriend and Commanding Officer—waiting for her out in the hall. Thanks to his audience of fellow Thrakorian soldiers and members of the Kings Guard, he was working hard to maintain his professional demeanor, rather than take her in his arms and check that she was okay like she hoped he wanted beneath that icy façade. Despite being a strong-willed and intelligent woman, Kyra felt weak after Kronus's harsh words and as though her determination to succeed and serve had truly been broken. More than anything else in the entire world, she wanted Thrayke to hold her. If only her lover could kiss away the tears threatening to fall and tell her everything was going to be fine. There was a part of her that hoped he would defy convention and soothe her obvious pain, but like always, they were divided not just by the social standards of their new society, but also by their separate races themselves. As usual, Kyra couldn't show him how much she needed his support in public because of her inferiority, and she despised Kronus and his regime even more for imposing a strict lifestyle and set of rules and laws on her and the other humans he evidently cared nothing about.

Even if Thrayke had asked, she didn't know where to begin explaining to him what'd just happened between her and his King and guessed he either had no idea what a douchebag Kronus was, or he'd learned to simply look the other way. Kyra figured it had to be the latter, given his years of loyal service to his reign. Thrayke had to know just how disinterested Kronus was in the running of his planet and she wondered why he'd even bothered bringing her to the Chief of Defense's headquarters to discuss her findings at all. Kronus didn't care about the increases in rebel activity and he'd seemed downright bored the entire time her Thrakorian commander had been outlining their discovery. In her opinion, their trip had been utterly pointless.

"General Millan," Thrayke said in a strange combination of a greeting and an awkward attempt at getting her attention on him. Kyra peered up into his intense blue eyes and had to fight back her tears when she saw the concern for her burning within them. He clearly had no idea just how awfully King Kronus had treated her and part of her was thankful he'd had no clue, for it meant he'd played no part in her belittlement. She was glad he'd always remained such a genuine friend since joining his Gentry and couldn't deny there was a part of her that felt bad for not having been fully honest with him in return. They'd been close for months after her arrival at The Tower and were now lovers, and yet she'd still never told him or anyone else about the night she'd first met King Kronus while he and his soldiers were in the throes of taking control of Earth and its inhabitants.

She'd spent every day since with a major crush on her sovereign savior and had somehow fooled herself into believing that he could still possibly be that kind, gentle man that'd pulled her free from the thorny rose bush as a child and kissed her better. Kyra had been just five years old at the time and had peered up into the face of a man she knew was unlike any she'd seen before, but at the time she hadn't known why. He'd given her hope and a sense of belonging and she often wondered if part of her childish mind had turned the memory of him into some kind of guardian angel. If it weren't for Kronus, she had no idea what might've happened to her on Invasion Day, or if she would've even survived the ensuing chaos in the aftermath of their attack. At the time, she'd had no idea their planet had been invaded by another species, but she'd later learned the truth, and how the man she'd been saved by was none other than their new ruler.

Kyra had then served his cause without question and had joined the Human Royal Armed Forces when she'd decided to pursue a career as a code-breaker and computer scientist. Not once had she had delusions that she might meet the King again, or that if she did, he'd remember her with the same fondness as she did him, and so she'd never believed her crush could become a reality. The dreams she'd had about him were never what'd driven her onwards and up the chain to her now high rank within the Gentry, but they'd fueled her confidence. Having belief in someone as all-powerful as King Kronus had been exactly what she'd needed to pluck the girl from the slums and make her believe she could earn herself a place within the human middle or upper-classes. Her crush had been a perfectly innocent infatuation for years and Kyra knew the escapism had helped her get through the tough times during her life thus far. Through her dreams, Kronus kept her hope of a better future alive, just like he had on that rooftop, when in reality he'd evidently forgotten all about her and the promises he'd made that night.

Realization struck her then. Kyra hadn't had much luck with men later in her teenage years, and guessed part of it had to be because she'd compared everyone to her imaginary savior. After a powerful yet too intense love affair with Silas, one of her commanders in primary training, she'd then sworn off men entirely and focused solely on her career. But, when she'd reached The Tower as part of her introduction into the Gentry, she'd met the incredibly powerful and intimidating Besieger Thrayke and her guard had come down thanks to the kindness and genuine interest he'd shown in her. Thrayke had wanted to know her. He had valued her opinion and encouraged her incredible mind where others had overlooked it in the past. They'd soon let themselves develop an emotional connection, before inevitably moving onto a physical one, and he'd never treated her as inferior to him, despite his high standing. He'd shown her a world still governed by their race's strict rules, yet given her a prestigious place among the Gentry because he'd believed in her, and together they were leaps and bounds ahead of anyone else when it came to deciphering the rebels' codes. She was truly enamored with Thrayke both intellectually and emotionally and was eternally grateful for how he'd helped her gain confidence in her skills and settle into her high-ranking role within the Human Royal Armed Forces. They weren't forever and they both knew it, but for now, she couldn't deny that what they had together was pretty amazing.

Thrayke had also shown Kyra just how much he cared and wanted to keep her around by instigating the administration of Lorde Greegis's strange test serum. The treatment had ensured both health and longevity to her life in a way human scientists couldn't even begin to imagine. In that one move, he'd added hundreds of years to her lifespan by pushing her to the top of the very short list of candidates, and now she was fitter, stronger, and far less breakable than she'd ever been before because of it. Still fully human, Kyra had been given the treatment as a test subject and it'd altered not just her body, but also her genetic code itself. Their technology had repaired holes and malformations from within her makeup, but the serum, its benefits, and existence were still so top-secret that her treatment had only been given under the proviso that she was sworn to secrecy about it for the foreseeable future. Kyra had often wondered how or why they'd developed the serum in the first place, and was even more dubious after Kronus's clear disinterest in her kind. There had to be something in it for them and she hoped that in time she might find out their real reasons for playing around with human DNA.

"Do you need me to debrief you, sir?" she asked, hoping Thrayke might take the opportunity to get her alone, but he shook his head no.

"No need, General. The craft is ready to take you back to The Tower," he informed her, and Kyra nodded. King Kronus had told her he never wanted to see her again, and to leave as soon as possible. It appeared he'd issued orders to that effect right after he'd stormed away. It was fine by her and she vowed never to romanticize the memory of that horrid man ever again.

"Yes, sir. I'll head down there right away," she replied, and saluted him. In public, Kyra knew they had to maintain their working relationship, so she hid her need for his comfort and approval, but was struggling. She couldn't bear to look into his eyes any longer, so turned to leave, but Thrayke grabbed her by the top of her arm. He leaned in close so as not to be overheard and peered at her through worried eyes.

"I don't know what happened in there, but I'll make sure you aren't accused of anything or punished because of it. I'll keep my word—the oath I made you. You can trust me to keep you safe," he told her quietly before letting her go. Kyra knew he was referring to when she'd finally opened up to him as they'd talked honestly together the day before. She'd shared her doubts regarding the Thrakorian leadership and their reasons for having come to Earth. At the time, she'd wondered if he'd brandish her a rebel, but instead Thrayke had listened to her deliberations regarding the cracks in the system and he'd promised to keep her safe regardless of her doubts. He hadn't confirmed or denied that her assumptions might be somewhat true, but his silence had led her to think maybe she wasn't too far off, and how perhaps all might not be as it'd once seemed.

Kyra climbed into the small hovercraft and was escorted back to London by the same group of Thrakorian soldiers she was sure were guarding her the entire visit to the Chief of Defense's stronghold. They'd gone there to discuss her findings in regards to the rebel gatherings, and instead of moving forward, Kyra now felt as if she'd gone ten steps back. The Thrakorian soldiers in the Kings Guard Service hadn't even listened to her describe how and why she'd made her discovery, or once asked for her input. When she was finally allowed to speak, King Kronus hadn't seemed overly interested in the markings she'd found leading them to the rebel gatherings, but at least he had still heard her out. It was only when he'd figured out she was the girl he'd saved back on Invasion Day that he'd turned nasty and she still couldn't figure out exactly what'd made him treat her so awfully.

Once back in The Tower—the headquarters for the human Gentry officers—Kyra ditched her Thrakorian overseers and went to her room. She fell into bed, feeling exhausted, and lay there, praying for sleep, but remained awake for hours. She mulled over everything that'd happened the past couple of days and when morning came, she knew exactly what to do. Work was the only cure to her melancholy, so she went in early and stayed late that day and the next.

Thrayke didn't return and his disappearing act only added to Kyra's anxiety over the whole situation, so she worked even harder to make sure she passed the time both busy and distracted. Within a few days, she'd worked so many hours she was pulled aside by one of her colleagues, who asked after her wellbeing and then immediately offered her a shoulder to cry on when she saw the pain behind her eyes.

"I'm fine, honestly," Kyra told the middle-aged woman, Trinny, and she was offered a scowl in response. She then fiddled with the buttons on her black combat jacket, aware that she might just be on the verge of an emotional meltdown. "There's a lot going on, and I'm pushing myself to get through the workload. That's all," she tried again, and then followed the intuitive woman's lead over to the window where they could talk privately.

"Our job is to protect the way of life millions of people out there have the right to live. But, that world means nothing if you're stuck behind a computer all day instead of living your own life," Trinny told her with a kind smile. "Never forget that we aren't mindless robots working behind screens depicting a virtual world. It's real. *We're* real. Life is for living as well as working." Kyra gave Trinny a little squeeze and felt herself well up when the woman hugged her back. She still hadn't been given any comfort since before Kronus and his harsh words, and although she'd never tell Trinny what'd happened to upset her, she still appreciated the gentle reassurance.

"You're right, thank you," she replied, and then went back to her work on the rebel markings she'd discovered, rather than the inane tasks she'd been plowing through over the past few days. Kyra looked over her findings again and recalculated the dates and coordinates based on the algorithm she'd now perfected. Her calculations got the same results as before.

One of the gatherings was only a few days away

in the Indian city of New Delhi. She was desperate to get a team out into the field so she could see for herself what was happening during the rebel meetings. Once there, she wouldn't need to act or put a stop to the gathering itself, but her findings there would go a long way to securing her evidence to their unconvinced sovereign. King Kronus wouldn't be able to deny her intel if they had concrete proof of insidious rebel activity, and Kyra went back to the drawing board, putting together a plan of action she hoped might get her on the ground as soon as possible. She knew it was dangerous to go against her orders to remain in The Tower, but at the same time, she didn't much feel like cooperating with her Thrakorian leaders, and with a profound return of passion for the task at hand, ignored the doubt niggling at her gut.

Once everything was ready, Kyra beckoned over one of her fellow younger officers, General Gage, and she showed him her findings. His eyes opened wider and wider as he read over her report and she knew he was on board before he even opened his mouth. "Fancy a trip to India?" she asked, and Gage nodded. He too was a fantastic code-breaker, and they'd already chatted a few times over her time at The Tower, during which they'd realized they had a similar approach to their work. Each of them had progressed through the ranks quickly thanks to their naturally sharp gut instincts, and even now, Kyra knew she had to trust the urge deep within her that said he'd make the perfect ally in this covert operation. It wasn't about proving anyone else right or wrong, but about demonstrating to herself just how right she had been in deciphering the markings, and she knew Gage was the man to help her.

"I have a contact in the dock who owes me a favor. I'll go see what's the protocol for booking a craft without the proper authority, or am I wrong?" Gage asked quietly, and Kyra knew her sly grin said it all. His assumption was entirely correct. They had to get to that meeting, and by any means necessary, but she didn't necessarily have the go-ahead from above. They both knew they'd need to work quickly and under the radar if they were going to sneak out of The Tower and get to India in time, so he didn't waste any of it questioning her further.

Kyra would deal with the backlash when they returned, but hoped the evidence they collated would provide them with enough of a reason to have gone unescorted in the first place. She just hoped Thrayke would hear her out when the time came to explain herself. "I think I'll tell her it's a reconnaissance mission, and covert. The Besieger has previously been involved in the case, so are you against me dropping his name into the conversation if we hit a snag?" Gage checked his facts before heading off to cash in his favor with his friend at the docks.

Kyra paused to think about it for a moment and hated how their actions might potentially cause Thrayke to be angry with her, but had to say yes. She was sure he'd understand eventually.

"Do what you have to so we can get that ship," she told him, and then watched as he headed toward the doorway. Things were going ahead and she was more than ready.

Kyra spent the time Gage was gone gathering some items she thought they might need, such as monitoring equipment, cameras, and decoders. She wanted a weapon, but knew a trip to the armory would raise too many questions, so figured they'd have to ensure they remained undercover right until the very end. A battle with potential rebels wasn't what they were after and Kyra knew they'd have to work hard to make sure they had the perfect cover—even if it meant going in unarmed.

With her backpack stuffed to the brim with equipment, she then grabbed a pen and paper, and began conjuring up fake identities for her and Gage. She decided, thanks to their similar age, that they would pretend to be a newlywed couple looking for somewhere to stay for a few days so they could celebrate their new marriage. They had to be wealthy enough to afford travel, but thrifty enough to have chosen budget hotels along the way, so she gave them complete backstories of being middle-class humans with decent jobs in the education sector.

After a bit of fooling around with one of the computerized systems to create the identities, she then grabbed a pair of invisible stick-on bands the undercover rebel-hunters often used. They were fitted with fake chips inside to overwrite the information stored in the chips inserted in every human's wrist, and she programmed them so that she and Gage then became Timmy and Kiki Paynter from New York City. She made sure they had plenty of credits to coincide with a story of travelling the world on their honeymoon, and added fake background histories with added details provided by the computer software to fool any hotel concierge that might like to check into their records.

By the time she was done with their bands, Gage had returned, and he had good news.

"All sorted. We're on a cargo craft leaving in twenty minutes, and Deena's logged us both as on exercise for the next week in case anyone looks us up."

"Did you have to get Thrayke involved?" she had to ask and felt a weight lift from her shoulders when he shook his head no. "Good, it'll be easier to explain this way. Put this on, *darling*," Kyra said with a smile as she handed him the wristband and they each secured them into place over their existing microchips.

They were then on their way with no time to

spare and she soon started to feel the excitement flaring in her belly. She'd never done something so reckless before, but knew it was the right thing to do. If King Kronus had only listened, he would've agreed, but instead he'd been so intent on telling her off that he'd forgotten the reason she was there in the first place—to take down the rebels threatening his reign.

He'd told her to stop her foolish servitude, but Kyra couldn't. It'd been engrained in her since Invasion Day and whether he wanted her to or not, she knew she'd fight for him until her dying breath.

CHAPTER TWO

After hopping from one ship to another, Kyra and Gage stepped off the cargo hovercraft the next day and into the glaring Indian sunshine. It was far hotter than she'd anticipated, but luckily they'd changed into light summer clothes while on the first craft, so were each much cooler than if they'd still been in their army combats. The pair fit into the civilian scene in no time at all, and Kyra was glad they'd gone over the roles each was playing in minute detail. She reminded herself that they were playing the part of middle-class humans with credits to spare, otherwise such frivolous travel wouldn't be possible. Gage was quick to exude an air of wealth that'd give the impression he came from an affluent family. In many ways, the character he'd appointed himself reminded her of Silas and his disregard for being careful with his credits, and she encouraged that element of his fake personality to shine because she knew that was exactly how the McDermott's acted. She hoped the hard work would pay off and couldn't deny that the last thing they needed was to be questioned about how a young couple could afford to travel the world.

They both knew it would be obvious they were tourists, but they played the roles of the happy newlyweds with ease. Gage slid his hand around Kyra's waist and pulled her close, whispering into her ear while she grinned and played the dutiful, blushing bride. They'd already discussed en-route how they would play up to their roles in whatever way necessary, and although part of her felt uncomfortable accepting kisses and affection from him, Gage never made her feel like it was anything more than an act. It was actually rather nice being doted on and Kyra let herself enjoy the closeness, but she also realized how much she'd missed Thrayke the past few days. She longed for him in ways she hadn't counted on, and hoped they might return to their comfortable closeness again when they both got back to The Tower.

She and Gage took a quick look around city and then checked into a strategically chosen hotel. While he secured the room, Kyra looked out the window onto the street below. She could already see some of the rebel markings on the walls below her perch and watched for a while as most civilians passed by them without even stopping for a look. When a man then stopped to check the time on his watch, but was also clearly checking out the symbol on the wall, she knew it was time to move.

"We've got one," she told Gage, and they quickly made their way out onto the street so they could follow their unsuspecting mole's lead. Before long, he ducked into a nearby bar, and they tailed him inside, but once they were there, they stayed far away from him and the men he went to meet with toward the back of the dim tavern.

Gage ordered two beers, while Kyra grabbed them a booth. He slid in beside her and gave his fake bride a kiss along with her drink, and Kyra grinned across at him while she twirled the wedding band on her finger.

"I was just telling the barman about our wedding," he told her, being careful to remain in character at all times in case of any eavesdroppers. "He told me I'm a lucky man, and I informed him of how I already knew," he added with a wink. Despite their act, she felt her cheeks burn.

"Of course you're lucky, not everyone gets to have such a hot wife on his arm," she replied playfully, and Gage laughed. Growing up, Kyra hadn't had all that much male attention, and any she had gotten wasn't always the sort she'd wanted or understood how to handle. Now though, she guessed she'd blossomed at last, because for some reason she'd often received flattering comments from the men she encountered, and still couldn't quite believe she was having a semi-relationship with one of the top Thrakorian military men, the Besieger.

There was also another reason Kyra had to guess was to thank for her recently discovered allure. As much as she hated Greegis, the scientist responsible for her new and improved state, she had to admit his serum had done wonders to her body. Her skin tone was now naturally even and the treatment had strengthened her nails and hair, creating silky softness the likes she'd never known before. The treatment had even given her a healthy glow no matter the late nights or stress she was under. Kyra two-point-oh was certainly an improvement, and she sometimes forgot about the added health benefits and longer life that were also afforded to her because of Thrayke's affection and his ability to pull strings where necessary.

Gage and Kyra then chatted quietly for a while and she enjoyed getting to know him a little better. He was a kind, sweet man, but underneath the gentlemanly demeanor she could tell he was also passionate and fun. When a song came on the jukebox that he liked, Gage quickly grabbed his 'bride' and swiftly began twirling her around in his arms. Kyra went with it, and used the time to cement their story as lovers in the eyes of the man they were both still watching from the periphery, as well as all the other patrons and staff inside the bar. For all they knew, everyone there could be rebel recruiters or activists, so they were acutely aware that things might turn nasty incredibly quickly if they were discovered in their deceit. "Timmy!" Kyra hollered when Gage dipped her and kissed her neck, making sure to use his alias rather than his real name. He didn't stop; in fact he simply spun her again and grabbed a handful of ass. Some of the men nearby cheered him on, and Kyra suddenly realized what he was playing at. By the time the song was over, they had the attention of everyone in the room, and before long, were chatting to lots of the men and women sat cradling their drinks by the bar.

"Kiki and I are after seeing the best sights New Delhi has to offer, what do you recommend?" Gage asked, and a few of the locals began offering him some names of hidden gems around the old city.

"Are you visiting New Delhi long?" the barman asked, and Kyra was purposely sheepish. She shook her head, but offered a half-shrug at the same time.

"A few days. We aren't staying in each stop long," she replied, and he smiled.

"Have you heard about the old temple on the outskirts of town? It has the best view of the city at sunset, you should check it out," he told her with a wink. Kyra knew full well that was where the rebel meeting was due to be held two evenings later, and she grinned back at him.

"Yeah, we had heard about that place. We were thinking of checking it out in a couple of days," she answered, and was careful to keep a cool head while she gave him an obvious signal that they were there to attend the gathering. He smiled, and it was clear that her assumptions had been right. The barman was one of the rebels, or was at least working with them, and he handed her a fresh drink, but said no more as he continued serving the other customers.

Kyra took a long swig of the refreshing beer and

was reminded of her time spent with Blue and the others in the hotel bar of The Crowned King in Los Angeles. She'd drank to try and hide from the pain of failing in both her private and professional lives, and the drunken haze had been a welcome release from her stress. She hadn't had much alcohol since then, apart from when Thrayke would open a bottle of wine he'd procured while they'd eat dinner together, but having a beer again was different. Wine was nothing more than a fancy accompaniment to dinner, whereas the lager brought with it a sense of fun and relaxation, but also memories of the hard time she'd had getting over everything with Silas. He'd tried to sabotage her career in order to keep her at Fort Angel with him, and would've succeeded if her Thrakorian trainer, Gron hadn't stepped in and saved the day.

"Penny for your thoughts," Gage asked from beside her, and Kyra quickly snapped out of her reverie. She hated that even years later the history with Silas could still get to her, but was glad it was all over with and he was long gone from her life.

She smiled across at her pretend husband and enjoyed the warm smile he gave her in return. It was easy to bask in Gage's affection, even if it was fake, and the past quickly melted away while she focused again on the mission at hand.

"Where are you going to take me tomorrow then, darling?" she asked as she snuggled into him, pressing against his tall body with her hips and breasts. She caught the sound of his breath hitching in his throat, and wondered if he was enjoying their role-play a little too much, but didn't step away.

"We're going for a walk around the old city, followed by lunch on the river and a tour of the old ruins," he told her, and she was pleased he'd chosen lots of open places in the city where they could check for symbols and markings that might prove useful in their final report.

"Sounds wonderful," she replied, and finished her beer before dragging him back to the makeshift dance floor for another twirl.

Before long, the entire bar was bustling with patrons, each of them eager for an end of day drink, and the pair of undercover officer's were soon chatting away with many of the other drinkers. They kept their subjects light and lied through their teeth about the places they'd supposedly visited on their trip so far. Having prepared their backstory, Kyra had been careful to only include places they'd each actually visited over the years, but she let Gage take the lead as he was the most travelled of the pair of them. He talked at length about some of the ruins in various European cities, and the vast Thrakorian skyscrapers he'd watched light up the nights' sky in Thailand. He was careful to include Kyra in his stories, and she did the same when regaling the group about her experiences in both Hawaii and Japan.

When last orders were called, she refused a final drink. She was already buzzing and didn't want to end up stumbling back to the hotel in a drunken state. Gage was chatting to two men by the bar, one of which happened to be the man they'd followed inside, and she was impressed at his ability to blend in. She left him to it, and opted to nod along absentmindedly while two women she stood with were talking away about how much they hated their jobs as cleaners at one of the town's agencies. Kyra listened for a while, and indulged in a little bit of the girly chatter when the conversation moved on, but wasn't really interested in hearing about how they'd found ways to whiten their teeth and had found a doctor willing to give them cosmetic surgery on the black market.

"You have amazing skin and teeth, Kiki. What's your secret?" one asked, and Kyra smiled. She would never tell them that she'd undergone a risky and still trialing treatment at the behest of her Thrakorian lover, or that it'd left her body in optimum condition with a lifespan of potentially hundreds of years.

"Lots of sleep," she lied, and used it as an opportunity to leave the conversation. "Speaking of, it's time me and my husband went to bed," she added with a wink, and the two young women giggled. Kyra joined the three men at the bar and greeted each of them warmly. She caught just the end of the conversation, but knew Gage would fill her in when they got back to the hotel, so didn't pry.

"We might see you both on Friday then?" one asked, and Gage nodded. He then shook hands with the man and turned to his fake bride. After kissing her deeply, they said their goodbyes and left the bar. Kyra giggled as he twirled her around the empty street and they danced their way back to the hotel and began wondering if Gage had indulged in one too many beers too.

"I actually had fun tonight, *Timmy*," she told him when they were alone in the room and had checked for bugs. "Did I miss anything good?"

"Just a direct invitation to the gathering from two of the recruiters," he answered, and was clearly very pleased with himself. Kyra grinned and told him about the barman's comment, and they both knew their plan was coming together at last. She then took a shower while Gage set up a camera to record any movement in the street below, and they both double-checked the vicinity for any recording devices or monitoring equipment. Thankfully, they were still clear, and so the pair went through the plan again and made their notes about what'd gone on in the bar that evening.

By the time they crawled into bed together, making sure to keep at opposite sides of the thankfully large mattress, Kyra was exhausted. The long trip and busy day were taking its toll and the beers weren't helping keep her eyes open either. Soon she was fast asleep and was dreaming of blissful nothingness before she knew it.

***

"Morning gorgeous," Gage said with a wide smile when she stretched and lifted her head from the pillow the following morning. He was dressed and ready to go and Kyra was shocked that she'd managed to sleep in.

"Hey, why didn't you wake me?" she asked, accepting a coffee from him.

"I did, but you cursed at me so I guessed you needed longer," he answered with a dry laugh, and Kyra joined in. "Such a lady," he teased, and she slapped him on the arm. Gage checked over the equipment again while she got dressed and tidied up her unruly hair with the help of a straightening iron. The shorter style was much easier to look after than her previously long locks, and before long Kyra was ready to go on their tour of the ancient city.

The pair of them wandered the streets at a leisurely pace, taking photographs constantly in an attempt to capture as much of the city as possible. They posed for passionate selfies, and took it in turns to capture shots of the streets, architecture, and of course, any rebel markers they found along the way. She hoped they were playing their roles in such plain sight that any onlookers wouldn't give them so much as a second glance, or question their choice of photography backdrops. Years of training had taught Kyra how not to stick out like a sore thumb, and she used every tool she had in her code-breaking box to turn it around and blend in effectively.

By that evening, they had hundreds of photos, and Gage backed them up while Kyra changed into a figure hugging dress for another night out on the town. They started at one of the clubs their new friends at the bar had told them about the night before, and it wasn't long until they were both chatting with civilians like the pretend couple of friendly tourists they were portraying. There were young men and women all over the old city, and she knew now that it was a bustling metropolis for the up and coming middle-classes. Kyra hoped that if she hadn't joined the army, she might've eventually found herself in a similar place to this in a business sector role, and found herself dreaming of the different life she could've had away from the strict regime she'd pledged her life to after leaving high school. In another life, she could've truly become like Kiki, and she had to wonder if it might've been a better or worse life without her new Thrakorian friends in it.

On their way back to the hotel, the pair stopped by the same bar from the night before for a nightcap, and were pleased to find a warm welcome awaiting them. Both Kyra and Gage made an effort to talk with the locals and other tourists again, and by the time they returned to their hotel, each had made up their minds.

"I want to attend the meeting," she told Gage, after they were sure the room was clear. "They trust us, and by the looks of things, there are far more humans interested in joining the rebels than we ever anticipated."

"I agree," he replied, and Kyra was glad. "This is bigger than we could've imagined, and these symbols were clearly meant for only the middle and upper-class humans to find. Those two recruiters—Andreas and

Marko—aren't looking for scumbags to fight for their cause. They're looking for clever, educated people to join them, and expressed a clear interest in the pair of us," he added. Kyra was pleased to hear it, and had noticed Gage talking quietly to the two men before closing time at the bar again. At the time she'd played it cool, but was happy to hear they had seemingly picked Gage out as a prime candidate.

Kyra kicked off her high heels and was just about to unzip her dress, when the door burst open, and an entire squadron of police officers stormed into their hotel room with their weapons held high. She spotted a mixture of humans and Thrakorian's in the team, but wasn't given the opportunity to ask any of them what was going on when she was forced down onto her knees. She was then stunned into silence when a face she knew well appeared from around the doorway. Silas's older brother, Tarquin stormed over to where the strong Thrakorian soldiers had them at the ready, and he scowled down at her. Their hands were then tied behind their backs, and each of them stayed silent while the officers took their places in a circle around them.

"Timmy and Kiki Paynter, you are both under arrest," he told them in a loud tone that she assumed was for the benefit of any other travellers who might've met them over the past two days and could possibly be listening in on the chaos.

Kyra was pleased to discover he wasn't keen on blowing their cover, and she nodded in understanding, then looked over her shoulder when she heard rustling from behind her. A human soldier was quickly packing up their equipment and notes, and he handed the pack over to Tarq. He then leaned down and whispered in her ear. "Anything else I need to grab before we go?"

"Wardrobe, there's a backup drive," she answered almost silently, and he quickly searched the small cupboard for the device. Once located, he stashed the drive and then nodded to his men, two of which grabbed the prisoners by their bound wrists from behind and pushed them towards the doorway with a forceful shove. Kyra played her role right until the doors closed on the police truck, and fought the entire way down the stairs and out into the street. She cursed and kicked at the hold the policeman had on her, and in the end, a Thrakorian soldier stepped in to take charge of their prisoner, as it seemed she was too much for the human one to handle. Once inside the van, she ceased her struggle and grinned at the man who'd initially led her.

"You kicked me in the nuts," he informed her, clearly annoyed that she was so pleased with herself, and she shrugged.

"Whatever. You should've been ready for a bit of a fight. Where are you taking us, anyway?" she asked, and it was Tarquin who answered from the front of the truck.

"Out of the city to a holding facility, just as we would with real rebel threats. We won't blow your cover though, so I hope you're ready to sit in cuffs for a few hours," he told her, and Kyra wriggled her shoulders before pulling her arms beneath her and around to the front.

"I don't mind at all," she answered with a smile, and then turned to look at him again. "So, who intervened with our mission?" she quizzed, and Tarq laughed loudly at her gall.

"Who do you think? He's meeting us there and then taking you two back to The Tower for debriefing." That shut her up, and Kyra sat back in her seat while Gage tried his hardest to wriggle his arms beneath him like she had. He seemed to be struggling though, and soon gave up.

Kyra knew they were in for a huge telling off

when Thrayke caught up with them, but she decided to do her best to ensure Gage wasn't punished for taking her on the mission that was all her idea. She'd make him listen to their findings, even if she had to take the brunt of Thrayke's anger first. They had conclusive evidence of immense rebel activity, and she wasn't sorry for having sneaked away in order to get it.

CHAPTER THREE

Kyra, Gage, and their team of police officers were barely through the door when Thrayke stormed over to intercept them. He was bristling with anger, just like she'd thought he would be, and for the first time she felt the true force of the hardened soldier and renowned warrior's wrath. He was terrifying, and so far all he'd done was stare her down. She trembled, cowering before him, and couldn't quite meet his gaze.

"Take them both to holding cells, and send an Inquisitor in to get this one's story," he bellowed, and chest poked Gage before he was led away.

"No, please don't interrogate him. It was all my idea," Kyra pleaded, but it fell on deaf ears. Thrayke wasn't entertaining any niceties, and he seemed intent on punishing them both for having put together a secret mission while his back was turned.

"She's with me," was all he said, not even looking at her. He then stalked away, and she followed behind him with Tarq and a couple of the others. When Thrayke reached a room at the far end of the hallway, he opened a door and ushered her inside, but then put up his hand to halt the others from following her in. "I'll take it from here," he told them, and after Kyra took a seat behind the huge desk she finally looked up at him properly. The daunting Besieger watched the men retreat, as though not wanting to be overheard, and her suspicions were confirmed when he then unplugged the recording system and pressed a button that she knew would deactivate the two-way mirror.

"Please just hear me out," she mumbled, but knew he wasn't in the mood to listen to her appeal. Thrayke marched up and down before her, and Kyra was becoming more and more uncomfortable as she watched him pace. "I did what I had to so we'd know for sure—"

Thrayke cut her off before she could finish her plea by roaring with such powerful rage that she froze. Kyra went to cover her ears, but realized her hands were still tied, so was forced to sit trembling in her seat as he bellowed. She watched him in shock, and knew she'd messed up tremendously. She'd never seen Thrayke raise his voice at all, let alone give out a pained war cry like that, and silent tears quickly fell from her eyes. Kyra didn't dare say another word, but held her head high regardless of her fear.

He slammed his huge hands down onto the table before her, and then wrenched the heavy metal desk up off the ground with ease. It went flying against the wall and broke into pieces, but Thrayke wasn't done. He trashed everything in sight, from the light fittings to the camera equipment still mounted on the wall, and eventually the walls themselves. He pounded holes the size of melons into the cement, while Kyra could do nothing but sit in wait for his rage to subside.

"You defied a direct order from the King," he eventually yelled, and turned to face her at last. Thrayke peered down at Kyra in the dim light coming only by the glow filtering in from the hallway now that he'd trashed everything else, and he then fell to his knees before her. His face was just inches from hers, and she could feel his panted breath on her face. "He'll have you punished for this, or worse, and I won't be able to protect you. Not from him. Why would you do this? Your covert mission is tantamount to treason…"

"No, he wouldn't do that," she replied, shaking

her head. She had to believe Kronus wouldn't hurt her, even though he'd treated her terribly during their meeting. "I told him I was correct with the symbols, and how I wanted to serve him. He said to leave it alone, but it wasn't an order." Thinking back, his words had been for her to give it up and go back to her other work, and the sinking feeling in her gut told her Thrayke was right to be so angry. She'd underestimated how Kronus's word was clearly always law, and immediately began to panic.

"He told me to get you in line or else send you away," he told her, and leaned in to kiss her cheek so delicately it was as though his outburst from just moments before hadn't even happened. His lips then trailed to hers, but he only gave her a chaste peck. "And he demanded I stop seeing you."

"What?" she blurted out, and grabbed his face as best she could with her bound hands. Thrayke pulled the cuffs free without batting an eye, and he then leaned into her hold for just a moment, clearly struggling with the order that he walk away, too. "He can't do that," she told him, but knew it was pointless. Of course he could, and for reasons she couldn't understand, it seemed Kronus was intent on making her life hell simply for having come back into his. "What will he do to me?" she had to ask, even if she despised his answer.

"All I know is that the Lawbringer is on his way to sentence you. He might even go as far as to order you to be killed for treason, or perhaps sent to the convict camps to serve out the rest of your days there. Either way, you'll potentially lose everything you've worked so hard for, Kyra." Thrayke wrenched himself away from her and sat a few feet away with his head in his hands. "What did you say to anger him?" he mumbled, and she could tell he was genuinely dumfounded by King Kronus's response to her visit.

Kyra slid off the chair onto her knees so she could shuffle over to him, and when Thrayke looked up at her, rather than hold him again like he clearly expected, she delivered the hardest slap across his cheek she could muster.

"You coward!" she cried, and then crumbled in defeat, folding in on herself. "All of this, I did for you. I did it because you made me promises and let me believe in this cause—in *your* King. He's a bored aristocrat and you're all a bunch of 'yes-men' who run his planet for him." Thrayke pounced on her before she could utter another word, and he pinned her to the floor using her arms and the sheer force of his powerful body.

"I suggest you shut your mouth right now, Kyra. You don't know anything about him or our cause," he shouted down at her, but still didn't deny that her words might be true.

"That's where you're wrong. I met him once, a long time ago," she informed him, and then smiled when his eyes widened. "Back when he cared and was kind enough to show it. He saved my life."

"You're the girl, aren't you?" Thrayke asked incredulously, and he paled, climbing off her. "The soldiers who escorted him that night were talking about a girl he found on Invasion Day, and how he saved her from being caught in a rose bush. It was the first humane thing he'd ever done, and probably the last. How hadn't I put it together when you told me the story before? And why didn't you just tell me the full tale of that night in the first place?"

"Because she never told anyone," a voice from the doorway answered him, and they both turned to look up at the man who'd joined them in the now devastated interrogation room. King Kronus stood in the beam of light streaming in from the hall, and he almost blocked it out thanks to his immense frame.

Thrayke jumped up to his feet and pulled Kyra along with him. They both stood staring at Kronus like he might be some shared apparition, and he gave them a few seconds to let his presence register. "Can I have a word?" he then asked, and Thrayke walked toward him.

"Of course, sire," he answered, but Kronus shook his head.

"With her," he corrected him, and while he wasn't happy, Thrayke seemed to accept the fact he had no choice but to acquiesce and leave them alone. He stepped out past the King, and Kyra heard him slam the door at the end of the hall closed in his temper. Kronus ignored his adviser's upset, and instead watched her intently. She could just about see him in the dark, and despite the fact he hadn't said anything, felt relieved that he'd come instead of the infamous Lawbringer.

Kyra hoped his presence meant he'd changed his mind, or at least come to pardon her misdemeanors, and she silently implored him to say something, anything. "He's right, you know," Kronus finally said, and she stepped closer to the light so she could see him properly. "You're the one and only kind deed I ever did. All of this," he indicated the facility, and she guessed he was referring to the entire world around them. "Was my soldiers' doing. They advised me how and why it was worth keeping you humans alive and in servitude, and have governed for me ever since. I honestly don't care what happens to your race, only whether or not my people survive."

"You have to care, surely?" she replied, and couldn't believe his words might be true, regardless of the evidence she'd seen. "What else would you do? Who would you lead if not this world you claimed? Your people forced us to accept the invasion, to praise you and your reign. And yet, just days ago you treated me like it was the most idiotic person alive to want to serve you."

"I lead because I was forced to accept this world from my father, not because I care a thing about your kind or this planet," Kronus answered with a sigh, and he held out his hand for her to take. Kyra hesitated. She didn't know if she could trust the man standing before her, and wondered if he was about to belittle or chastise her again. Everything about the way he looked, so huge and powerful, yet gentle and kind, reminded her of Invasion Day, and it was confusing being in his presence again. She'd dreamed about that moment her entire life since, and remembered how scared she'd been, however he'd calmed her. She was just as terrified now, but didn't find comfort in his presence the second time around. "Come here," Kronus whispered, his hand still outstretched.

"Am I to be punished?" Kyra asked, but he remained perfectly silent and still rather than answer. His hand was still stretching out towards her, and she got the impression he wasn't used to being made to wait while his subjects deliberated or asked questions. "Are you going to send me away like a convict, or am I to die in the desert like a rebel?" There was still no answer from the god-like creature standing before her. "Why are you here if you don't care?" Kyra was ranting, she knew, and still he seemed intent on not answering. His command to go to him hadn't changed, and neither had his stance. King Kronus was a conundrum all right, and she was conscious of how no amount of second-guessing was getting her anywhere. Kyra realized that she craved what his outstretched hand offered her more than she could say, and without another word from him, she eventually gave in. Like that child she was last time, she yearned for his support and the safety his hold promised, and just like she had on Invasion Day, she took his hand and let him pull her out of the shadows into his embrace.

He wrapped her in his arms and gave Kyra a hug

like she'd never felt before. Kronus's body was so tall and wide against hers that she couldn't get her arms around him to fully return the hold, and so tucked her hands around his waist and gripped the sides of his dark shirt. She was trembling uncontrollably, and guessed it was all to do with the whirlwind of emotion she was currently feeling. Being close to him was wonderful, but it also made her crazy with worry and confusion. She couldn't understand his body language or guess his moods, and knew he was something so far out of her league she might never be able to. "Why do you care?" she whimpered against him, and she heard a deep sigh fill his lungs as Kronus breathed her in.

"With you, I can't help but care. While I couldn't understand it, I knew I couldn't stay away once I found you again," he whispered to her. "You...infect me. I feel warm and worthy in your presence, like I'm ready to take the world from your tiny shoulders and carry that burden as my own, but also as if I failed you profoundly by even letting it weigh so heavily on you in the first place. I'm sorry I was so awful before, but you genuinely caught me off guard and that doesn't happen—ever." Kyra couldn't fight her shock at his intense explanation, but had to admit he'd helped her understand a little better and she was glad he'd decided to be so honest.

"You were so mean," she mumbled into his chest. "All my life I've taken pride in serving the man who saved me on that rooftop, and I did it out of respect and..." she paused, but forced herself to be honest as well, and to admit her feelings toward him at long last. "And love."

"There's nothing lovable about me, Kyra. The sooner you realize that the better," Kronus told her, and released her from his grasp as though she'd offended him again. Kyra knew then how he had a habit of lashing out rather than face his emotions head on, and could tell he was doing the same as he'd done at that meeting. Kronus couldn't handle her expression of adoration for him, just as he hadn't handled her initial outpouring of devotion, and so was pushing her away again. This time though, she was onto him, and didn't let it upset her. "You won't be punished for defying me, but I'd better not hear about you gallivanting off on secret missions again," he added, and she simply nodded. "Go back to The Tower and carry on with your work. That's where I need you, not out here among the rebels where you might get hurt."

While she was glad to be allowed back to normal work, Kyra couldn't help feeling like he was telling her goodbye again. Their eyes met and he held her gaze, just as they had in the Chief of Defense's skyscraper. This time, she finally saw through the pretense and could see the emptiness in them, as well as the lack of drive or purpose in his life. No matter how awful he'd been, she still cared tremendously for this huge beast of a man who seemed emptier than anyone she'd ever known, and Kyra genuinely didn't want this to be the last time she saw him.

"Will I ever see you again?" she asked, not dropping her eyes from his.

"I doubt it," he answered with a shrug. Kyra hated how he could switch from warm to cold so quickly, and silently cursed his aloofness. "Just do your job and stay safe. I won't offer you anything more than you already have. I couldn't even if I wanted to."

"In that case, I'd better let you go back to your tragic, empty life with nothing but yourself for company," she retorted sharply, and knew she was overstepping the boundaries again, but couldn't help herself. It was her turn to be angry, and if he was allowed to lash out, then so was she. "I take it you know about me and Thrayke? Well, if you and I are nothing, I'll continue seeing him as long as I want, which might be for quite some time thanks to the serum your scientists gave me."

Instead of pleading his case or ordering her around, Kronus grew visibly colder, and Kyra's confidence shrunk along with her resolve. She stepped back against the wall, but it was no use. He leaned in closer and stopped only when they were nose to nose. He dominated the air around them both, and her chest tightened as she began to panic beneath his icy stare.

"He so much as touches you again and I'll kill him with my bare hands, is that understood?" Kronus said flatly, and she didn't doubt it for a second. "He took you for that treatment sneakily, but I let him off because it was for his favorite 'pet' in The Tower. If I'd known then that it was you…" he tailed off, and Kyra looked up at him in utter disbelief.

"You'd what? Refuse him? Let Greegis kill me?" Kronus slammed his hand against the wall beside her head, but then cupped her cheek with the same hand in an odd gesture of dominance and gentleness.

"I would've made them wait rather than risk your life on an unstable serum. I don't think you realize how dangerous it was," he answered gruffly.

"I know full well, and almost died on the gurney," she informed him, and suddenly felt lost. "You're making me crazy. I don't know what you want from me, Kronus. Either let me be part of your life or let me go, you can't have it both ways."

"I can't be what you want me to be, but I can't bear to think of you with another either. I want you locked in that Tower behind a computer screen until the end of time. I can't have you, but I'll die happy knowing no one else can have you either."

"That's incredibly selfish, and old-fashioned,

don't you think?" Kyra asked, and he raised an eyebrow in question. "You don't even know me or want to be with me, yet you're ready to lock me away because something inside you is drawn to me. I make you feel something for the first time in your life, and instead of enjoying it, you're fighting that sentiment every step of the way. I thought your race treated women equally, or perhaps it's only the Thrakorian women you respect?"

"Watch your tongue, Kyra. Don't forget with whom you're talking to," he warned, growing colder again, and she knew for sure she was right about him. Every time she pushed his buttons Kronus retreated emotionally, but she knew she had to say what was on her mind while she still had him there. She couldn't live her life being controlled and forced into loneliness by a being she'd never see or have in her life, yet who ruled everything about her shackled existence. There had to be a compromise, otherwise Kyra knew she'd never be happy.

"I'll never forget, don't you worry," she said, and placed her hands on his shoulders. "I'll never forget the man who gave a little girl with nothing to live for a simple kiss on the cheek, and a glimmer of hope. I kept that hope so close to my heart that I spent everyday since with a secret love for the King who many followed because they had to, but I followed because I wanted to. I never believed in true love or that you might have felt something for me in return, but if you truly do—then let me live my life."

"Thrayke won't give you a future, Kyra," he told her, and stepped back to lean against the opposite wall.

"I don't want a future with him, I just want to keep his friendship. He and I were friends before anything else, and I couldn't stand it if you took that away from me," she said, and meant it. If they couldn't be lovers then she'd have to accept it, but she still wanted his friendship and the connection they'd shared since she arrived at The Tower.

"In a way, that's worse," Kronus replied sorrowfully. "I want to know you like that. To understand what makes you tick, make you laugh and bring you gifts I know you'll love."

"You're right, you don't know me, and you certainly can't have it both ways. For both our sakes, decide now," she implored him, and felt incredibly overwhelmed with sadness. Kyra knew she was about to lose everything that made her something different than the other mindless followers of their regime. He wasn't going to back down, she could see it in his eyes, and knew the answer before he even said the condemning words.

"Get out of that damn dress and go back to The Tower," Kronus said, and he then stormed off out the door and towards the entryway at the end of the hall. Kyra looked down at herself and quickly realized she was still wearing the tight dress she'd worn out in New Delhi with Gage. It was far from the usual army attire, but she'd had to wear civilian clothing while undercover so hadn't had a choice. She didn't care what she was wearing or whether he liked it, and she certainly wasn't finished with him yet. After kicking off her borrowed boots in a huff, she stormed after Kronus, but he was gone. Kyra let out a surprised humph when she walked through the door and bumped straight into one of the huge Thrakorian Sentinel's who'd been part of the earlier extraction team.

"The Besieger would like a word," he told her, and then quickly ushered her into one of the other interrogation rooms. Kyra sighed angrily, but knew she had no other choice than to comply. After a deep breath, she followed his lead, and tried not to look around at the others in case it was obvious just how broken she felt inside. Kyra was unsure where Kronus had gotten to, and she kept telling herself she didn't really care. It was no use, but she still had to try. The soldier closed the door behind her, and Kyra hovered, unsure how best to proceed.

"General Millan, please have a seat," Thrayke said in the same authoritative tone she'd grown used to while in work, and she expected to find someone else in the room with them, but quickly realized they were alone. She did as he asked, and stared across the desk at the man she'd shared many intimate moments with, and yet who now regarded her like nothing more than another of his Gentry officers. "You and General Gage are on probation until further notice. The King doesn't wish to pursue a court martial, but any more insolence may result in future punishment. A hovercraft will be here shortly to take you both back to The Tower. You're dismissed."

If she'd felt broken after Kronus's words, she was utterly in pieces under Thrayke's cold, hard scrutiny, and wondered how or if she would ever come back from the two life-changing conversations she'd just had with both powerful men in only one day. Kyra suddenly wanted nothing more than to be alone. She needed to grieve the loss of her connections to the men she'd put her trust in, and whom had both seemingly tossed her aside so easily. Tears pricked at her eyes without warning and she wanted to fall to pieces, but instead she forced her head to take control of her body, rather than her heart. Thrayke's iciness broke her heart, but the strength she somehow always managed to summon in times of need rose up within. Just like when she and Silas had ended, she forced her tears away, held her head high, and climbed out of her seat without a single word to the man sitting opposite.

CHAPTER FOUR

Kyra thundered out of the small room and walked right into Tarquin. He was the last person she wanted to see while she was fighting back tears because she knew he'd see through her façade, but it seemed she couldn't avoid his questioning gaze. He grabbed her by the shoulders, holding her still.

"What's going on?" he asked, but she couldn't say a word. Kyra ran straight for the ladies' bathroom, where she locked herself inside and flung her dress off and onto the floor in a huff. She had no clue what on Earth was going on, which was the only part of this entire situation she *was* sure about. After turning on the shower and climbing in, Kyra let it run as hot as she could, and was grateful for the cascading water and billowing steam that hid the tears that forcibly returned. Before she could calm down or begin to reason with herself about what'd just gone on, the all-consuming sobs she'd fought hard against showing finally came bursting out of her, and she had to grip the bar on the wall to stop from falling to her feet.

Kyra tried to take stock of her life, and to figure out exactly where she could go from here. King Kronus had finally found her again, but had refused to let anything between them flourish, no matter how much they both seemed to feel a connection to one another. She'd settle for friendship with him, but wasn't even offered so much as a snippet of a relationship. He'd told her twice now to leave him alone, and so she vowed she'd do just that. He might be her leader and King, but Kyra was determined not to let him rule her heart or her soul any more. Her entire life, she'd held onto this dream that they had shared something special on that rooftop. Something different to anything she'd known before or after Invasion Day. Kronus had been more than just a crush or a memory held so dear it'd warped into something more. They'd affected one another profoundly, and he couldn't deny that even if he had denied his feelings or desire for her.

And then there was Thrayke. He had been a friend and mentor. He'd protected her and listened to her hopes, dreams, fears, and secrets during their time together, but now he was like a stranger, too. He would never defy his King, and so Kyra knew they could never be anything more than colleagues ever again. She was alone, again, and felt so empty in the knowledge that she was heading back to The Tower to live a boring, lonely life. And all at the command of a King who refused to acknowledge her so Kyra hated that she would never again be allowed to enjoy the company of the enigmatic Besieger.

Her tears ran and ran, refusing to be quashed any longer, and she cursed herself for foolishly letting the two powerful Thrakorian men affect her so incredibly. A quiet, polite cough then alerted her to the presence of someone else in the bathroom, and Kyra poked her head around the curtain to see who it was. Tarquin was stood there, holding a fresh set of combats for her to put on after her shower. His face dropped when he saw her expression, and he shuffled his feet awkwardly.

"I thought I'd locked the door," she moaned, and then pulled her head back under the water to avoid his pitiful gaze.

"You had," he answered over the roar of the shower. At least she hadn't imagined that. Kyra couldn't deny though, she was glad he'd brought her a change of clothes, and realized she hadn't thought that far ahead when she'd stormed in there. She listened out for the door closing shut behind him, yet he seemed intent on not leaving her alone, and his voice carried across the jets to her again. "There's been a development. You're needed in the control room."

"I'm off the case, Tarq. I'm only good for sitting behind my desk like a good little geek I'm expected to be. Apparently field-work isn't for sweet little naïve girls like me," she snapped, and turned off the water with a huff. Kyra dried off and wrapped the towel around herself, and opened the curtain to find him still standing there waiting patiently.

"I think anyone who's ever met you knows you're worth far more than that," he replied with a sly smile, and his cocky expression took her right back to life worlds away from where they were now. She hadn't seen Tarquin in years, and felt like a completely different person to the girl she'd been back when she and his brother Silas had started dating. Back then, she was just a Corporal at the end of her primary training. His mother had looked down at her like a scummy little foster-kid who was so obviously trying to get her hands on her families' fortune and status, but now Kyra outranked them all, and she hoped Freya McDermott knew all about the success she'd achieved after ditching her precious son. "Stop letting other people define who you are, or what you're worth. I don't know what's gone on, but I do know you're better than this. You're not the girl who goes crying to the bathroom while men walk all over her. You're the girl who punches the man holding her back in the face and walks away with her head held high." His words startled her, but they did the trick, and he had her grinning from ear to ear within seconds.

"Oh, so you know about that?" she asked with a

laugh she hadn't thought she'd be able to share so soon after being so upset, but Tarq's words were already making her feel ten times better. They'd hardly gotten to know one another while on vacation in Hawaii, but had developed a quick and easy playfulness back then that still seemed there, despite her having moved on from her relationship with Silas a long time ago. After he'd purposely tried to hold her back from completing secondary training in the top-five, thus losing her recommendation to go for Elite training, she'd done exactly as Tarq had just said. Silas was so desperate not to let her go that he'd hurt her both mentally and physically, and she'd responded with a punch to the face before walking away and never having seen him again.

"Absolutely. He came clean after that Gron guy sent him to work at a training camp in the middle of nowhere. He lasted two weeks before calling our parents and begging them to do something. Father managed to get him reinstated at Fort Angel, but under one condition—he became Sentinel Gron's personal lackey." Tarquin laughed at his brother's foolishness, but seemed impressed at the same time, and Kyra wondered if perhaps the strong hand had been exactly what Silas had needed. Lieutenant Psy had given him many chances to change, yet he'd always seemed to resort back to his selfish ways, but evidently not under a Thrakorian's tutelage. "Gron's a beast, and has really put Silas through his paces, but he needs it."

"He sure does," she agreed, and then had to smile thinking of her old trainer. "Gron kicked my ass on more than one occasion, but I needed it every time. I needed this, too. Thank you," she added, and he bowed slightly. He might not have known what'd upset her, but she appreciated how he wasn't bothered about prying into her personal affairs. Tarquin only seemed to care that she was okay, and now that he was satisfied, he turned around so Kyra could get dressed and ready to head back into the fray.

"Anytime, midget. Anytime," he replied, and laughed when she shoved him on the shoulder. "You ready?" he asked without looking back. She checked her appearance in the mirror, and was grateful for the wondrous serum and its rejuvenating benefits. Kyra hardly even looked puffy or red-eyed. In fact, she looked downright bright and bubbly, even if she didn't feel it.

She hummed in affirmation, and then followed her kind friend back out into the thankfully far less occupied hall. They walked in silence, and Kyra was grateful for a few minutes in which to try and clear her head. She didn't know what'd happened in the thirty minutes or so she'd been in the bathroom, but if whatever development was potentially about to halt her and Gage's return to The Tower, she knew it had to be important.

Tarquin led her through another maze of corridors and walkways, before finally opening a door to a computer control room. Numerous consoles were set up to monitor both the site they were at and the local community, and Kyra was shocked to find one of the screens filled with a face she'd come to know well over the past few days. Tanner, the barman from New Delhi, was taking quietly into a handset with one of the Thrakorian soldiers, but the sound of his voice was being pumped into speakers all around the room so that the others could hear what he had to say.

Kyra spotted Thrayke over by the wall, and was surprised to see King Kronus standing beside him, along with his personal guard, the Master Protector. They were each watching the screen and listening intently, and were like huge statues against the dark brick. Kronus was taller, but Thrayke was bulkier, and together the duo reminded Kyra of the gods of old that were always depicted as powerful warriors. Each had their own strengths and weaknesses, and yet they exuded a clear and concise message that they were two men not to be messed with—ever. Kyra felt drawn to them both in many ways and despite them having said they felt the same in return, they each wanted nothing to do with her. *Aren't I lucky?* she thought as she crept inside.

"What's going on?" Kyra whispered to Gage when she reached him, in an attempt to force her thoughts away from the two behemoths in the back of the room. She'd sought out and joined the only person she wanted to go to in the small crowd, and was genuinely glad to have found him there.

"Tanner's an undercover soldier. It turns out he's been working on a similar theory as us for a while now, but hasn't managed to get in with the rebels before this round of gatherings. He's made contact to discuss what went down with us last night," he whispered back, and Kyra nodded in understanding. She was pleased to find they'd had a friend there all along, but now had to assume their cover must have been blown and their progress lost.

"Talk among the locals is rampant, and they know the two newlyweds were carted off by soldiers, but they don't know why. Rumors are rife about it being either rebel activity, an illegal marriage, that they were on the run, or even that Kiki is a slave who ran away from her master to be with Timmy," Tanner's hushed voice echoed all around them, and suddenly all eyes turned to her and Gage. "This story has created a real buzz, and I'm sure it'll be a topic of conversation at the gathering tonight. It's a shame they can't be here, as I'm sure Tuka and the others would've accepted them after all of this." She'd heard that name, Tuka, and knew he was the head rebel recruiter for that area. He was their original target, but since being carted off, their objectives had been forcefully changed. If only there was another way.

"Why can't we be there?" Kyra blurted out before she could stop herself. "We'll say the police had nothing on us and we passed the Inquisitor's interrogation, as technically we still hadn't done anything wrong. Rebellious thoughts don't necessarily mean treason," she asked the group, and her gaze met Thrayke's. He was the only person she'd ever confided her doubts about the Thrakorian regime in, and he'd promised to keep them to himself for her protection, because fundamentally they'd seemed true. Kyra was glad to have had the opportunity to remind him of that promise, even if it was in front of a room full of soldiers. "The pair of us can head back to New Delhi, albeit a little worse for wear, and we'll go to the gathering with one heck of a story to tell about how badly were treated and how much more determined we are to join the rebels because of it."

"Absolutely not," both Kronus and Thrayke answered in unison, and everyone turned to look at them in surprise. Tanner waited patiently from behind his device, and Kyra wondered if he knew who'd just spoken or not. He still seemed his usual calm self, whereas everyone in the room was visibly uncomfortable around the King after his so uncharacteristic outburst.

"It's the most logical approach, sir," she replied with a sneer. "Gage and I can go in, attend the meeting, work with Tanner to gather intel, and he can then feed it directly back here. We'll go only as far as we need to before coming back, and it'll give us an inside view of their regime in a way we've never managed before."

"She's right," Tanner added, and she liked him all the more for it. "They can say they were held for questioning and nothing further."

"A word outside please, General," Thrayke then said, and he walked over to the doorway, which he held open for her. Kyra had to resist the urge to roll her eyes, but followed, and was surprised to find Kronus tailing behind her as well. The three of them stood in the hallway together, and she peered up at them both in anticipation for her telling off. It didn't take long before they each started yelling at her for even daring to suggest going back undercover, and she stared back and forth between them both in a daze. Their words were pouring over her, but she didn't care to listen to either of their demands and orders. It was their faces she was watching, noticing as their cheeks were getting redder and redder as they bellowed. Both were going on and on, and she suddenly began laughing.

"An hour ago you both walked away from me. You each told me to stay out of your lives, and now you suddenly care? How dare you!" she cried, filling the stunned silence. "This is the logical approach to gaining intel and a pathway directly into the rebel hold. There's no reason for me not to go, so unless you're planning on locking me up…"

"If that's what it takes, I will," Kronus interjected, but Kyra shook her head. It was all suddenly so abundantly clear to her, and so she used every tool she had to try and get her own way. Her relationships with them both were lost anyway, so she figured she might as well go out with a bang.

"But then you'd have to explain why, and something tells me neither of you want your dirty laundry being aired in public. If I'm to be the secret you're both so ashamed of being found out, then I'm going to do as I please, and you aren't going to stop me," she called his bluff, and it worked. Kronus and Thrayke both looked at each other, and couldn't deny that neither had a leg to stand on if they were serious about putting a stop to her continuing with the mission. They would have to give a reason for saying no to what was a sound strategy, and so one or the other would have to come clean about how she'd gotten too close, and that she'd reaped the benefits along the way.

Kyra doubted Kronus would allow rumors about his private life to circulate, so Thrayke would have to take the heat. Not only would that cause outrage among the older human Gentry because of his favoritism, but also he'd likely have to step down from his post as the Besieger. After Kronus's insistence they stop seeing one another, she hoped the King wouldn't appreciate them being expected to remain a couple for appearances sake after the dust had settled either, but also hoped she might never find out just how far he was willing to go to keep her as his spinster minion.

Kyra gave it a few seconds of tense silence, and then poked her head around the door to call to Gage. "We're on, I'm going to get ready." He nodded in acceptance, and she saw Tanner grin on the screen across the way.

A second later, she was walking away from the two huge Thraks that'd tossed her around like a ragdoll for the past half-day, and she was glad to have her head held high and her confidence firmly back in place. Kyra reached the bathroom she'd showered in and was fishing her dress out of the laundry bin she'd flung it into when the door opened and in strode King Kronus.

"Don't ever talk to me like that again," he warned, and the fire in his eyes both excited and scared her. "You and I are going to have a little chat when all of this is over, mark my words."

"That's good to know. Thank you, sire." She knew she was pushing her luck, but she'd had enough of the ups and downs of his moods, and wasn't ready to play his games again just yet. Now, he was saying he would see her again, whereas before he'd said the polar opposite. She was getting whiplash with all the back and forth. "If you'll excuse me, I need to get back into this damn dress."

Kronus was on her in a heartbeat, and her breath left her in a rush as he pinned her to the lockers. His hand fisted her combat shirt at the waist, and the material quickly gave way beneath his powerful grip. Kyra heard the shirt rip, and felt the bottom few buttons pop, but she still didn't cower before him. She didn't care about the shirt, only her pride—which had been damaged enough for one day.

"You're not just a dirty little secret, Kyra. I want you back in one piece, do you understand?" his gruff whisper sent a shiver down her spine, and she nodded while peering back up at him.

"Then please stop treating me like an inconvenience. Take care when you handle my foolish emotions, and me, or there'll be no going back. I get that you're not used to taking a leap of faith, especially with a human, but please learn to trust me," she quietly pleaded, and Kronus nodded against her cheek. He took a deep breath, as though breathing her in, and then stepped away.

"I'll try," he said, and then left her to get ready in privacy.

***

Tarquin and the other policemen dropped Kyra and Gage off at the outskirts of the ancient city a couple of hours later, and they tossed her backpack to the ground before speeding away. They'd taken the equipment and left them with only their clothes and essentials, plus the small camera they'd taken their snaps with, but the squad had already gone over the plan at length, so Kyra and Gage both knew it was wise to get rid of their surveillance kit. They would liaise only with Tanner, who would relay the information back to the others. No recording equipment or monitoring devices would accompany the pair of covert operatives, as it was agreed by all that the rebels would undoubtedly be checking for them. Thrayke hadn't been keen on them going in there without any backup, but they all knew that in order to properly blend in, they had to rule out anything that might put them at risk of being caught out.

They both looked bedraggled, exhausted and in need of a wash, and had done so on purpose to ensure they looked as though they'd just spent the night in the interrogation cells. Kyra knew their hotel room would've gone to other travellers, so they headed straight for the bar where Tanner was already in the process of setting up for the daytime shift.

"My word, what happened to you two?" he asked, feigning ignorance and concern for their wellbeing. He then ushered them inside, and gave Kyra a hug to soothe her supposed upset. She guessed she must be playing her part a little too well when he held tight, and realized after a look in the mirror that she actually did look as if she was on the verge of tears. It wouldn't surprise her if she managed a few droplets with ease after the night she'd just had, so in one way she was glad for all the topsy-turvy emotions that were evidently still keeping her adrenaline pumping.

"We're fine, but I could do with a splash of hot water and something to eat if you can spare it?" she asked, and Tanner immediately showed them through to the back where his small living quarters were. They didn't say a word about the mission in case of eavesdroppers or bugs, so she and Gage maintained their cover even while showering and then sitting down to eat together. Kyra was well aware that they had to go right back into character, but this time it took her a while to shake off Kronus's cryptic speech about how he wanted to see her again after the mission was over. She wondered if he'd said it in a way that meant she was overdue a serious telling off, or if instead he was planning to lure her away so they could spend some time getting to know one another like she and Thrayke had once done. That basis of friendship had been a much needed connection for the pair of them. It was the foundation of their relationship rather than attraction and she hoped she might be able to have that with Kronus as well once the dust had settled.

"Kiki? Did you hear me?" Gage asked, and Kyra forced herself back into the room with an apologetic shake of her head. "We need to head off now if we want to make it in good time. Are you ready for this?" he asked, and she nodded.

"Thanks for the hospitality, Tanner. We're heading out for a walk, so will see you later," she called as they left the bar a few minutes afterwards, and he waved them goodbye with a smile. He'd decided against going to the meeting himself, seeing as they'd been handpicked to go by the rebel recruiters, but he had insisted they come back straight afterward to fill him in and make their final report, and they'd agreed, but knew it'd all depend on how the evening went. It went unsaid between the three of them that Kyra and Gage were willing to go with the flow where necessary to gather more intel, but their superiors back at the holding facility didn't necessarily need to know that, and she was glad to have discovered such a tremendous ally in Tanner amidst the covert chaos.

Gage led the way, and before long they'd reached the old temple on the outskirts of the city. Half of it had been ruined on Invasion Day, but parts of the epic temple remained intact, and what was left had been preserved by the local humans to create a stunning piece of architecture that many enthusiasts had made sure would last for many years to come. A guide was waiting by the entrance, and thanks to Marko's direct request that they attend, Gage knew exactly what the man was going to ask before he even opened his mouth.

"Good evening, would you like to join one of our tours?" he said warmly, and Gage nodded. "Excellent. North or southbound?"

"I hear the northbound views are lovely this time of evening," he answered, and the man smiled. He handed Gage a map of the ruins, and directed them to a small structure far off in the distance. Any legitimate travellers would know that it was the opposite that time of night, and opt for the southbound route to watch the sunset, so it was the perfect code for getting everyone who was there for the same reason in one place securely.

With a gentle smile, Kyra took her fake husband's arm and together they walked the length of the ruins to the northern edge. They then took their place among the small crowd already gathered there and greeted the others politely. Many of them they already recognized from the bar.

"I'm glad to see you evaded imprisonment, Timmy," a deep voice spoke from the crowd, and Marko, the man Gage had been speaking with a couple nights' before, stepped out to greet them. "What happened to you last night, my friend?"

"Marko, I'm glad to see you again, too," Gage answered, and shook his hand with a polite nod. Beside him was another man Kyra recognized from the bar, and he too seemed impressed to discover that they'd gotten away from police custody relatively unscathed. "They tracked us down after our contact in Thailand gave up our names, and it appears he was working as an informant," he then told them, having known full well that the story added up thanks to their insider knowledge.

"Were you interrogated?" the other man asked, whom Kyra realized had to be the infamous Tuka, and Gage nodded. From what Tanner had told them, he was not only one of the highest ranking rebel recruiters in the area, but also commander of the local faction, and so a worthwhile adversary within the treacherous group. Gage looked down at his unusually quiet pretend wife with a sad smile, and gave her a squeeze. Kyra had remained silent on purpose, and knew she was playing the role of the timid human scared stiff by her recent run-in with the law perfectly when they all turned to look at her with gentle, sorry gazes.

Tuka stepped closer and put a hand on her shoulder to draw her eyes up to meet his. Kyra did, and she was chilled to the bone by what she found there. Tuka had a hardened stare and a vast degree of iciness to him that shone out from behind his piercing blue eyes regardless of his sorrowful front, and his shaved head only added to the intimidating look he seemed to effortlessly suit. He smiled, but it was clearly forced. "It's okay, Kiki. I bet you were scared, but you know now just how strong you need to be to stand up to them. They're ruling our planet through totalitarian methods, but masquerading behind the pretense that they came here to save our species. You'll learn the truth very soon, and you'll be better off for it," he told her, and leaned in so close she wondered if he might kiss her cheek, but then seemed to think better of it. Instead, he lowered his voice and whispered in her ear. "Will you stay after the meeting's finished? I'd like to introduce you to some more of my colleagues."

"It'd be our pleasure," Kyra answered him, and his satisfied smile made her want to vomit. There was something incredibly off about Tuka, and she was quite sure she didn't want to end up alone with him any time in the near future. He reeked of affluence and power, but there was something else there, and she wondered if he might have his fingers in some very dark and dangerous pies as well as a high standing among the rebels.

When it was clear everyone who'd wanted to attend had arrived, Tuka and another man she hadn't seen before stood before the crowd of what Kyra estimated to be around forty humans. The pair welcomed them all, and then Tuka began quietly outlining why they'd been requested to attend.

"Many of you were personally invited here tonight, but others were clever enough to follow the trail of crumbs we laid out, so well done. Regardless of how you came to be here—we're incredibly glad you did. I have an important question I like to ask the people I meet nowadays, and it's simply…how's life? Any who answer with a, 'good, thank you,' or similar response are not worth my time, but any who check over their shoulders before answering me honestly, they're who I'm looking for. All of you were the latter. You appreciate the truth and have expressed your agreement in our beliefs that we've been conditioned to follow these aliens blindly. So many of us believed the propaganda they've fed us about why they're here and what they want from us, but it's all crap. We're here to both enlighten you, and to ask for your help," Tuka told the gathering. He was unmistakably a force of nature, silencing the crowd while alluring them with his rousing speech, and Kyra had to admit, he was impressive.

She leaned into Gage's hold even more, and he held onto her tighter. She hated hearing the blasphemous words that were pouring out of the man's mouth, but also despised how they also made fundamental sense. She'd raised concerns of the same nature to Thrayke once upon a time ago, and knew for sure now that the rebels really were targeting a more shrewd selection of the human population with talk of how they knew better. The new breed of rebels evidently counted on their ability to question the things that seemed out of place, and they were keen on utilizing that rare quality.

Murmurs of agreement echoed all around them, and for appearances sake, Kyra looked up into Gage's face and nodded to him. When she looked back to the front of the crowd, she saw Tuka watching them, and was certain by the self-assured look on his face that they had him fooled.

"We mean to seek out the truths hidden from our race and then bring them to light. We need you in order to do it. You are not rebels, but you will help your race survive by providing information and support when called upon by your handlers. This initiative is looking for those strong enough to play both sides effectively, and those who we can trust to handle the burden effectively," the other man continued. "Are you ready to properly save the human race from its oppressive ruler and his army? Do you consider yourselves worthy of a place in this regime? Would you give us your loyalty in return for a chance to change history alongside the men and women who've dared stand up to King Kronus and his race of brutes?"

Cries of affirmation came from the crowd around them, and Gage was quick to offer his service to the rebel forces with a throaty cry. Deep down, Kyra wanted to storm forward and snap Tuka and the other man's necks, but outwardly she maintained her cover. She grinned broadly and gave her fake husband a deep kiss rather than call out, and by the time she pulled away, many members of their small crowd were starting to fire questions at the two speakers one-to-one. They wanted to know more, and quite rightly so, and she listened in on as many conversations as possible to gather her intel for the debriefing she and Gage knew was coming the following morning.

The fake newlyweds then both made the effort to chat with some of the other attendees while they waited for the gathering to disperse, and Kyra began making mental notes of names and home locations of those they spoke with. It was a strange experience chatting to seemingly loyal, normal people, who deep down seemed intent on the ultimate demise of the Thrakorian reign, and Kyra had to keep reminding herself that her betrayal was a lie. Her heart was still mending after her strange few hours with Thrayke and Kronus in such close and intense proximity, but she knew that no matter what, she would always remain loyal to them. It didn't matter if at times her allegiance faltered; she truly believed that she'd always go back to what she trusted in, or rather whom. The innocent child within was still holding onto the hand of that soldier who'd saved her on Invasion Day, and she was starting to realize she always would.

Before too long, Tuka and the other man headed back through the crowd giving out small devices while explaining what they were to each of their new spies. She and Gage were one of the last to be given theirs, and Tuka took his time explaining how to use the small device, which Kyra recognized immediately as a primitive cellphone handset with which they could contact the rebels.

"Speed-dial one, and a voicemail system will answer. You simply need to state your name for recognition purposes, and you'll be called back within a few minutes. Only call when you have solid information you can give us, or have something to offer. We need to know you're committed to working for our cause," he told them, and then put his hand on Kyra's shoulder again. Tuka eyed her up and down, and leaned in close. "You seem a little more yourself, are you feeling better?" he asked, and she had to stifle her shudder.

"Yes, thank you. I guess I was a little freaked out after our arrest last night, but now I'm already feeling stronger and more determined to right the wrongs done to our race. Your speeches were very emotive, and I know without a doubt that I want to help take them down, in whatever way I can," she answered, and her belly ached with the lie.

"That's exactly the point of these gatherings," Tuka told her with a smile. "We need people like you if we're to succeed. In fact, I'd like to offer the pair of you an extended invitation for this evening, if you're up to it? We're off into the heart of the city to meet with some friends and celebrate tonight's success. Would you both care to join us?" Kyra looked up at Gage for his answer, but was sure they had no other option other than to say yes. Tanner was waiting for them back at the bar, however they both knew this was an important opportunity to check out behind the scenes of the rebel operation, so had to keep their handler waiting while they gathered as much information as possible.

"Count us in," Gage answered for them both, and they each followed Tuka back towards the entrance to the old temple. The far smaller group chatted on the way, and Kyra purposely started coming out of her shell a little more, as though loosening up after her scary night spent in the cells. She let herself smile and laugh along with her escorts, and Gage did the same. By the time the group reached what looked like nothing more than a small home in the heart of the city, she was back to being the happy-go-lucky newlywed she'd been playing just days before, and Tuka seemed positively taken with her.

"Are you ready to have your minds blown?" he

asked them, and then led the way inside. They followed, and Kyra gasped when she saw what entertainment awaited them within.

"I thought prostitution had been banned?" she whispered to Gage as she looked around at the scantily dressed humans inside. They were openly selling their bodies to the men and women who'd been invited along to what she guessed must be a brothel, and he nodded.

"Nothing's unattainable if you're wiling to pay for it," Tuka told them, evidently having guessed what she was whispering about, and he directed the pair further into the back of the house. "Those of us with the ambition and drive for it can have whatever we want, and that's why places like this exist. We house, feed, and clothe these men and women, and in return they provide a service needed as much today as it was thousands of years ago. None of them are forced, in fact they seek us out because they love what they do and want to share it with the world."

Kyra felt sick, and finally understood what it was she'd sensed in Tuka earlier that evening. He was nothing more than a criminal mastermind of the new world, and he wasn't ashamed about it one little bit. She suspected that the only reason he disagreed with the Thrakorian reign might simply be because he was a leader as well, and he wanted the recognition he felt he deserved. Tuka was a small-time predator in a pool of bigger, better, and more powerful creatures, and he didn't seem to like being overshadowed. He evidently wanted power of his own and to reign supreme in his territory. Rather than selflessly helping release the humans from their current ruler, Tuka was a clear example of someone who wanted to overthrow King Kronus in the name of a greater good, only so he could have that throne for himself once empty.

CHAPTER FIVE

"What can I tempt you with?" Tuka asked as he took a seat in the huge armchair that was unmistakably his position of power amidst his sordid dominion. Young women offered them various drinks and drugs, but they politely refused. One of his beautiful slaves then brought Tuka a tumbler containing what appeared to be a concoction of ingredients, and he took it without so much as a thank you to the young woman. He tossed the contents back, but they were clearly hard to stomach, and Tuka looked positively nauseous for a few moments until whatever was in the cocktail kicked in. He then visibly relaxed, and indicated for Gage and Kyra to join him on the chaise to his right. "All you need to do is ask, and anything can be yours," he added, eyeing them intently.

"But at what price?" Gage asked as they sat, and he earned himself a dry laugh from their host.

"You've already paid with your promises to serve our cause, dear boy," was Tuka's eventual reply. "But I wouldn't say no to some quiet time with your beautiful bride if you were willing…" He leaned forward in his chair to stare at Gage intently, and shooed the other women away. "Tell me, how old are the pair of you?"

"Twenty-three," Gage replied, as though actually entertaining the idea of offering her up to him for a moment, but instead of panicking, Kyra trusted in her comrade not to put her in harms way. She played along and kept her cool, and knew he'd never actually allow her to be used in that way. Her patience paid off, and Gage quickly shot down their host's request. "As much as I'd like to pretend I'm open to sharing, I'm afraid I cannot. Kiki's mine, and has been since I took her innocence. Understood?" he added, and the authority in his tone and intense stare as he regarded their new friend even scared her.

Tuka laughed again, and slapped his knee in appreciation of Gage's show of dominance. Kyra couldn't deny, she hated how men loved having their foolish contests to establish control over one another, and was instantly reminded of how Kronus had downright demanded he prefer her be alone and miserable than happy with someone else.

"Now, now gentlemen. That's enough of that," she chimed, and then accepted a shot of vodka from the waitress who'd returned. She threw it back in one, and regarded the men with a coy smile. "We aren't interested in entertaining anyone but each other, thank you. Your hospitality has been wonderful, however I think it's time we were going." Kyra stood, but in a surprise move, Gage didn't join her.

"Answer me this, Mrs. Paynter. When was the last time you let go of all your inhibitions?" Tuka leaned across to the small table before them, lifted another shot from the tray, and held it out to her. "There's a secret behind your eyes, and I'm dying to discover what it is. Perhaps you love another man, or maybe your lover is another *species* all together?"

Now then, aren't you intuitive, she thought with a hint of a smile. Kyra took the shot from him, sat back down, and drank it. "My secrets are mine to keep, but I will tell you that they've led me to places and people I could never speak of. I've seen things I doubt you've even dreamt about, and they are what led me here today."

"You're truly ready to question the life you've been taught to believe is right?" Tuka grilled her further.

"I already do," she answered, and raised her freshly refilled glass when he grinned at her and lifted his in a toast.

"Then you're already well on your way to phase-two. Tell me, what's the worst thing you've seen or experienced at the hands of our alien leaders?" he enquired, and in a move that surprised her, she answered honestly.

"My best friend, and her unplanned pregnancy that was taken care of in the most absolute way. I'll never forget what they did to her," Kyra told him, and a real tear fell onto her cheek at the memory of her old friend Brona's awful time during training. She'd gone to the Medical Division to take a pregnancy test, only to end up with a hysterectomy and therefore lifelong infertility. They'd been told it was an unavoidable consequence to an infection she'd developed, but Kyra truly believed otherwise. Tuka leaned forward and rested his chin on his hands with a solemn look in his eye, regarding her intently.

"We've had the same. One of my girls went missing after she attended a local clinic, but I'd taken measures to track her years before—like with all my girls. I followed the signal out into the arid lands, and found nothing but desert." He shook his head in clear disgust.

"Where was she?" Kyra had to ask. It was a question that had plagued her for years, and the thought of finding an answer suddenly overtook her need for intel about the rebels themselves.

"Buried beneath the sand in a mass grave, along with hundreds of other women. Their bodies had been dissected and dismembered, but none bore any sign of pregnancy, nor did any have a child's bones still within them."

"Do you think they're taking them away? Testing them? But for what reason?" Kyra knew she was blurring the line between the fake role and her real personality, but she had to find out as much as she could about the Thrakorian testing facilities and their purpose. She was also reminded of Colonel Summers, the cadaver in Lorde Greegis's lab. No matter how hard she'd tried to forget seeing that body after he'd received the same serum she had, Kyra couldn't fight her fears that there might be more going on than she'd ever know.

Kronus would never tell her. He could barely express any emotion at all, so it seemed she would have to settle for gathering stories from scumbags like Tuka if she were ever to know for sure.

"I don't think, I *know* they are. They're controlling overpopulation, but also taking people as test subjects for some reason. We cannot infiltrate their facilities yet, but there's something going on that involves stem cell research and genetic alterations. That much we're already sure of."

Kyra's heart sank. The exact serum Tuka was talking about had been given to her to cure any and all human diseases and add potentially hundreds of years to her life, and she shuddered as an icy chill swept down her spine.

"The babies, do you think…" she couldn't finish her sentence. The sheer thought that it might be true was too hard to put into words.

"Yes, I believe they're part of it in some way. And for their sakes, I have to find out why."

They stayed for a few more hours, and Kyra drank far more than she'd intended to when they'd first set foot inside the dingy brothel. She watched as the men and women sauntered around, serving drinks to their clients or leading them to the small dance floor for an intimate embrace, and she was surprised to find that they genuinely did seem happy there. Food and drinks flowed readily, as did many other mind-altering substances, but she steered clear of those.

After another deep and intense conversation, Gage eventually took her hand and led her over for a dance, and he commanded her body in such a way she was left panting for breath in his arms. He was so domineering it was a surprise, and Kyra giggled against his mouth when he leaned down to kiss her.

"You're drunk, and far too innocent to be in a place like this," he whispered in her ear. "Many men and women have their eyes on you, especially Tuka, so I'm thinking it's time we left—don't you?"

"Spoil sport," she teased, but nodded in understanding. It was all very well getting close to the rebels, but another thing entirely to become involved with them too much. Kyra knew it certainly wasn't safe to get in too deep. The pair were officially there to observe, infiltrate, gather intel, and then leave. They'd already pushed their time limit by hours, and she knew the team back at the police facility would be waiting impatiently to hear back from them. "Take me home, you naughty man," she then added, and made sure she said it loudly enough to be overhead. Gage kissed her hard and grabbed the back of her neck so he could fist her hair in his fingers, claiming ownership one more time before their host's eyes.

"I'll show you naughty," he answered with a sexy smile, and then dragged her back over to say their goodbyes to Tuka and his entourage. He didn't seem pleased that they were calling it a night, but they all knew he couldn't force them to stay without overstepping the very boundaries they'd laid out in order to attract them into the cause in the first place, so he soon conceded.

He handed Gage a card, and Kyra could see it had nothing but an address embossed on it.

"Tomorrow night," Tuka said. "Let me show you more of this world I've created, and what you can both have if you only ask for it."

"Until tomorrow," Gage answered, and he stashed the card in his pocket before they left. They remained in character the entire walk back to Tanner's, in case of spies, and Kyra loved being wrapped in the arms of someone who doted on her, regardless of her knowing it was all fake. The city slept while they took the long walk back, and she realized she quite liked being undercover. Having a role to play, with its rules and everything planned out, was easier than dealing with her real life right now, and part of her dreaded going back.

***

"Morning you two," Tanner chimed cheerily when they finally crawled out of bed later the next morning, and Kyra groaned when he pulled back the drapes so the bright sunshine hit her directly in the face, but there was thankfully no hangover, and she knew she had her serum to thank for that. "You were back late," he added in a carefully cheerful tone, but his angry expression told them both they were in trouble.

"We went to a party," was all Gage replied in answer, and Kyra simply hummed in affirmation as she poured them both coffee and grabbed a couple of rock-hard muffins Tanner had somehow managed to throw together and then ruin while they were still asleep.

"What's the news then? Are you two heading home this afternoon like you'd planned?" he asked, eyeing them warily.

"No, we've decided to stay a couple more days if that's cool?" she answered, and Tanner raised an eyebrow. This was not the plan, and they both knew it.

"Sure," he said in a deadpan tone. He then scribbled something down on a scrap of paper and handed it to her. *But you explain it to your boss.*

"Sure," she repeated, and focused on soaking up the alcohol in her system rather than explain. She could feel both of their eyes on her, and decided she wasn't in the mood for her interrogation quite yet. Kyra headed back into the bedroom, where she took a shower and let herself take time getting ready.

Eventually, the two men came to find her and dragged her down into the basement, where they each stripped down to their underwear and walked through a scanner to check for any bugs. Each of them were clear, and once they were on the other side of a solid metal door, they climbed into a set of combats each and loaded up the computer systems Tanner had set up at the ready so they could liaise with the team back at the holding facility.

"Do you realize how worried everyone was about you both?" Tanner finally said what was on his mind as the machines booted up, and Kyra turned to face the screen rather than listen to him rant. She logged in, loaded the messaging software, and then waited for someone to be ready on the other end. It was mere seconds before Thrayke's face appeared on the screen, and he was clearly angry with her, too. *What else is new,* she thought, and chose to ignore his scowl.

"Good morning, sir. Are you ready for our report?" she asked timidly, but knew he wouldn't be in a position to ask her any personal questions anyway. Thrayke had no other choice but to remain professional in his response because of their audience, so she used it to her advantage.

"Yes, General. I must stress, however, that you're hours late with your intel. Did you encounter any problems along the way?"

"No, in fact it worked out better than we'd anticipated. Tuka invited General Gage and I to a property of his in the heart of the city, where he filled us in on some of the illegal activities he and his comrades are overseeing. I have my full report here, and will send it to you now," Kyra replied, and she sent him the electronic file with hers and Gage's accounts of the evening on them. She hadn't lied about any of the details, nor had she hidden her findings. Thrayke would read it and know, just like she did, how the human rebel hierarchy were indeed onto the facilities experimenting on humans, and that they were getting closer to discovering exactly what scientists like Lorde Greegis were getting up to inside them.

"Very well. You are to return to base immediately," he ordered, and she could see his jaw clench when she shook her head no. "You have your orders, General. Return here immediately."

"No," she answered, and she heard the two men behind her take sharp intakes of breath. "With all due respect, sir, we've had an incredible lead and want to stay one more night to see where it takes us. I'll report back tomorrow."

Thrayke was livid, and he slammed his hand down on the table beside him. The sound came through the speakers so loud it made her jump. Despite there being a handful of men with him in the control room, the room behind Thrayke was all of a sudden deathly silent following his outburst, but she didn't cower or back down.

"Get back here, now. This time I won't hesitate to call in the Lawbringer to put both you and Gage on trial for defying direct orders. The sentence for that is a minimum of five years in the convict camps."

"We'll head back right away, sir," Gage stepped in, and Kyra cursed. Thrayke nodded and ended the call, and Gage grabbed her shoulders, shaking her. "Are you mad? Who do you think you are, talking to him like that?" he cried, and she realized that even Tanner was watching her wide-eyed. Kyra understood then just how close she really had let herself get to Thrayke since she'd arrived at The Tower, and how much she'd taken that complacency for granted. Right now though, she honestly thought that leaving was absolutely the wrong thing to do. If they left, the lead would go cold, and the questions still burning in her gut might never get answered.

"What Tuka was on about—the human testing," she said, staring pleadingly into Gage's eyes. "It's true."

"How do you know?" Tanner interjected.

"Because I've had it done on me," she answered, and he took a step back in surprise. Gage let go of her shoulders and did the same. He rested his hip against the counter behind, and looked Kyra up and down as though looking for some proof that what she was saying was true.

"Were you the one who got pregnant?" he asked, clearly remembering her story from the night before. Kyra shook her head.

"I'm the one and only person on the planet who was given the serum they're working on—or whatever the hell that stuff was—and lived to tell the tale. I need to know what they know and how, otherwise I'll never be able to live with myself for having accepted such a diabolical treatment."

CHAPTER SIX

Gage began spewing profanities, while Tanner paced the small room. They were both clearly taken aback by Kyra's revelation, but she wasn't sorry for having given up her secret to them both. It'd been hard keeping it to herself, and she felt like a weight had just been taken off her shoulders, especially after hearing that her race's stolen unborn might be being used in conjunction with the serum she'd been plied with. That same serum had given her terrible hallucinations and almost killed her, so she knew it must be something pretty immense if it could do that to someone while effectively trying to heal them of any potential illness and elongate their life at the same time.

"You two go. Now, before the Besieger can do anything to stop you. I'll tell them Tuka came here while you were packing up and gave you no other choice other than to go with him. But get your asses back here before dawn, is that understood?" Tanner instructed them, and Kyra grabbed him tightly while grinning from ear to ear.

"You wonderful man, thank you," she replied. "This is going to be worth every second, I can feel it in my bones."

Gage still wasn't impressed, and had no qualms telling her so, but he still went along with her. En route to Tuka's second choice of venue, he only grumbled a couple of times about how this was more than he'd bargained for when he'd signed up for their secret mission, and Kyra let him have his say. He deserved far more than just her appreciation, and she decided she'd make sure he was accredited with the success of the mission if and when the time finally came.

They arrived near to where the address Tuka had given them way too early, and didn't have a good enough reason to go knocking on the door hours before they were supposed to, so instead the pair took up residence at a nearby coffee shop. Rather than be tracked using their fake microchips to purchase their drinks, they instead worked off their order and had soon whiled away the hours until it was time to go and meet their formidable new friend.

Kyra changed into another of her sexy yet sophisticated outfits, while Gage opted for a professional looking shirt and tie combo that really looked good on him. "I could eat you up in that outfit, Timmy," she told him with a wink, and was glad to see the playful side of him return when he grinned back across at her.

"I'd eat you alive," he replied quietly, and Kyra laughed as she took his arm, before heading over to the strange new location with their fun and madly-in-love personas firmly back in place. The place looked just like any other house in the city, much like the brothel had the night before, but the presence of numerous security guards on the door provided a vastly different dynamic to the relaxed and welcoming vibe they'd previously received from Tuka and his men.

Kyra was just about to give one of the burly guards her fake name, when he stepped aside and opened the door for them without a word. Evidently he already knew who they were. Tuka was inside, along with his usual entourage of rebel soldiers and leaders dressed as civilians, and a handful of what Kyra assumed must be some his favorite employees she'd met the night before.

"Welcome to my home," he told them, and a stunning young woman offered the pair a glass of champagne. Kyra hadn't seen such lavish existence of corruption and power in all her life as she had the past few days, but gladly took what was offered to her despite her previous reservations about Tuka and his lifestyle.

"Thank you for having us," Gage replied, and the newlyweds followed their host through to a huge dining room where a meal fit for King Kronus himself awaited them. Tuka offered Kyra the seat directly to his left, and she took it with a gracious smile. He was being warm and generous again, but she didn't trust it for a moment, and knew he was assessing them both while playing the part of the perfect host. His eyes burned with secrets she knew she might never dare to learn, but her intrigue was too overwhelming to ignore. Tuka had the answers to everything she hadn't risked asking aloud her entire life, and she was drawn to that knowledge like a mouse to a poisoned square of cheese. She knew going forward would have potentially disastrous consequences, and yet she was willing to proceed regardless. She was ravenous for the truths only he seemed willing and able to provide.

Kyra chatted with Tuka for a while, and ate in abundance the many foods delivered to their table, some of which she'd never seen or even heard of before.

"I want you both to stay here now, as part of my team. What do you say?" he eventually asked, dispensing with the small talk, and the room went silent as the men and women around them listened for their answer.

"It would be an honor," Gage answered, and he finished his glass of wine while he mulled over the rest of his response. "But I assume that means relocating?" he asked, and Tuka nodded.

"Of course."

"Well then, first we have to go back to New

York and pack up our old lives. We'll leave first thing tomorrow and be back by the end of the week."

"Oh, well then that's such a shame," Tuka replied, pouting his lips to make a show of displaying his disappointment. "This is kind of a now-or-never deal, and I was so sure you'd accept. Perhaps I was wrong about you…"

He leaned closer to Kyra, and she made a point to stare back into his domineering gaze with her head held high. She was sick of being told what to do and where to do it by Kronus, Thrayke, and even Gage. She yearned to have the ultimate knowledge at her disposal at last, but also to have discovered it without their help. There was so much more she had to learn than what they'd so far been afforded, and her gut instinct told her that Tuka was the man to give her the rest of what she craved.

"If we're worth all this effort," she said, and waved her hand to indicate the lavish meal and planning that'd clearly gone into their evening. "Then you can wait a few days, I'm sure?" she asked, and included a flutter of her long lashes for added effect.

"You drive a hard bargain, Mrs. Paynter. You'd better make it worth my while," Tuka replied with a sly smile. Kyra leaned forward slightly, giving him a glimpse of her cleavage, and he bit his bottom lip as an almost inaudible hiss escaped him.

"I'm sure you won't be disappointed," she whispered.

"Very well then," Gage interjected before their host could try anything more on with her, and Kyra jumped in her seat at his authoritative tone. She then let her pretend husband take her hand atop the table, and leaned away from Tuka so that she turned her attention back to Gage. Kyra knew he was playing the dominant card again, and she was glad he seemed able to do it so well. He and Tuka were butting proverbial heads left, right, and center. She knew it was only a matter of time before something kicked off between them, so figured it'd be better if she didn't stir either of them up by coming across as too flirtatious. She had to stay on Gage's side, while wooing Tuka enough so he might reveal some of his truths to her before she ran off back to reveal all to their Thrakorian leaders, and just hoped she was doing everything right. The consequences of playing the game wrong could be disastrous—even Kyra knew that.

After the meal, the party retired to a small room towards the back of the house, where they lit cigars and drank whiskey poured over chipped ice. Kyra joined in, and wasn't once treated like she shouldn't be there by Tuka and the other men he associated with in his close-knit group of comrades. It all still very much seemed like a man's game, all the plotting and talk of rebellion, but she held her own during the conversations, and never once shied away from talking about the more difficult areas of their new and seemingly horrid world.

"What's your Invasion Day story?" Tuka asked her when they'd been left with a far smaller audience a little later on, and Kyra's hand immediately touched on the cross shaped scar on her cheek. She wanted to curse herself for inadvertently drawing attention to her scar, but knew it was already too late.

"I hid with some other children while soldiers killed our friends, families, and neighbors. We ran, and I fell down a ridge into a mess of barbed wire. I was taken to a hospital and patched up, and then taught to believe the events of that night were for my own good—just like all the other children my age. Now, I can see the world in a way I never imagined I might see it, and it scares the hell out of me," she answered, and found it scarily poignant that her fake story had somehow been tinged with a lot of half truths. The two lives she was living, but thought she'd kept separate, suddenly seemed to be merging, and it worried her more than she'd ever imagined. "I never saw any of them again—my friends. I always thought perhaps they'd gotten away, but now I wonder if their bones are just another set in another mass grave."

"More than likely, I'm sorry to say," he replied, and brushed the scar with his fingertip as he mulled over her tale, and he then began telling her his story. "I was a cocky teenager, and was so sure I could fight off the invaders. My friends and I picked up whatever weapons we could find and headed straight into the fray. They all died, and I dropped my gun. I hid, like a coward, and let the Thraks take me away. I then let them rule me, like all the others who had no choice but to comply. I was ashamed of myself for a long time, but not any more. Surviving that night was the best thing I could've done in resurgence, because now I can fight them in ways they won't ever see coming."

"How?" she asked hopefully, and leaned a little closer.

"In time, my dear. You need to be patient, but you'll learn the truths as you go," he replied, and kissed her cheek tenderly. Kyra blushed at his gentle touch, and sighed. She hated how fast the night was passing, and wanted time to stand still so she could carry on asking Tuka her questions.

"Kiki, it's time to go." Gage was standing a few feet away with a hard stare, and she instantly noted that his lips were pursed so hard she could barely see them. He was furious.

Kyra knew full well that when they left they'd never return again, despite what they'd promised Tuka. Thrayke would never allow her out of The Tower again once she was back there, and she begrudgingly stood to join her pretend husband. They said their goodbyes and then strode to the front door, where she let Gage walk ahead of her. Kyra hesitated with her palm pressed against the door handle.

"How?" she asked Tuka again, turning to look over her shoulder at him, and he grinned mischievously. He seemed to know exactly what she needed from him, and it appeared he was the first person who finally seemed ready to give her it.

"Shut the door, and I'll tell you."

She looked out onto the street where Gage had just turned to look back at her, having realized she was no longer right beside him. He was clearly surprised and concerned, but all Kyra could do was watch from the doorway. She wasn't satisfied enough, and felt incredibly conflicted about to what to do next. Truth, freedom, and the promise of knowledge and settling her debts to humanity were stopping her from stepping over the threshold, but at the same time, she knew she shouldn't stay. She shouldn't want to stay, and yet...

"Will you help me leave all my questions behind? Can you finally help me figure out what I'm missing?" she asked Tuka, but stared out the door at her comrade. She was on the verge of stepping out to join him, but was still torn. The doting follower and loyal soldier inside of her wanted to leave and obey her commander's orders. And yet, something private and previously docile was roaring deep within. It was a voice she'd never listened to before, but one that promised true independence and a chance to learn the facts for herself if she listened to it. She would never be truly free, but with the truth at her disposal, Kyra guessed she might at least sleep a little better at night.

"I'll answer everything I can, and help you find the answers to the others. Together we can do great things, if only you'll walk away from the old you and embrace the new." Tuka stepped a little closer, and she could feel his eyes burning holes into her back.

Kyra didn't say a word in response. She simply closed the door on Gage and his wide-eyed expression, and turned to face her host.

She didn't want to be Kyra Millan any more. She wanted to be no one, Kiki if she must, but she certainly didn't want to be ruled by any man or Thrak. Desire burned within for knowledge, regardless of how frayed she knew she'd undoubtedly end up because of whatever answers she found. Right or wrong, she knew she had to stay and see her mission through to the bitter end.

"Let's get one thing straight. I'm not staying to be another one of your *employees*, Tuka." She looked to her side where one of his stunning girls stood holding a tray of drinks, and he followed her gaze before focusing again on her face. "We're colleagues, friends, and nothing more. Is that understood?"

"Loud and clear, but it won't stop me from trying to woo you," he answered with a sly smile, and he held out his hand for her to take. She took it, and then walked back to the den with him, while trying her hardest to ignore the commotion behind the door where Gage was clearly trying to get back inside. She wanted to go back and tell him to stop, to go to Tanner's without her and let Thrayke know she was sorry. Kyra wanted him to tell Kronus that she simply couldn't be what he wanted her to be. However she couldn't tell him any of those things. There were so many things she hadn't been able to say to both of her powerful allies, and it hurt her chest just thinking about them, so she pushed them all aside. She wouldn't explain herself to anyone, and so wandered the house by Tuka's side in stunned silence at what treacherousness she'd just committed.

Despite her guilt, Kiki was there now, and she wanted answers. She would be strong, confident, and ruthless in her pursuit of knowledge, but also wise when it came to making decisions. Kyra would let her take control for a while, and she hoped with all her heart that it'd been the right decision.

"Tell me what you know about these testing facilities," Kyra asked Tuka later that night when they were sat together in the dim den, and for a while he did nothing but watch her with apparent interest. "You don't get to be vague, not after everything I just gave up at your request," she added, reminding him of what he'd promised on that doorstep.

"I only know the stories I've been told, but I'm happy to share them you. I want your intuition and knowledge to help us both find the truth I know we can, if we work together. Will you be what I need? Can I count on you to find and document everything we'll require if we're to piece together one mass account of the truth?" She nodded. Kyra wanted that more than anything else.

"That's all I want," was her answer.

"Good. Well, we've pieced together a few stories so far, and our own experiences led us to the discovery of that mass grave I told you about. Others have slowly come forward, but many are too scared to tell us just how bad it really is out in the slums of the cities we've visited. That's where we need someone like you. Someone caring, enigmatic, and trustworthy. These are the accounts we have so far," he said, and passed her a notebook half-filled with scraps of paper and a few scribbled entries. "You can be our scribe, Kiki. Fill this and as many other books as you can with the truths as told by the civilians we meet, and I'm positive that once collected, they'll help us piece together the answers that could potentially help us take down the Thrakorian's at long last, or at least their government."

Deep down, she knew she still didn't want to take Kronus down, but she didn't say so to Tuka. She had her own agenda, and as hard as it would be to discover the truths hidden in the various stories, Kyra knew she had to, and accepted the notebook from him, as well as the role within his regime. The mission had now become far more personal than she'd ever planned, but for her sanity, she knew she had to see it through.

CHAPTER SEVEN

King Kronus finished reading the latest report, shut down his computer, and then walked slowly out into the hallway of his vast mansion, where he began pacing up and down. Every inch of his body was screaming in rage, yet he was purposely poised and calm in his fluid movements, rather than lash out. He had no doubt that if he let himself blow, the home he'd spent almost twenty years refining would be reduced to rubble in the wake of his outburst, so forced himself to stay calm. The mammoth man knew the extent of his strength, and was always careful not to let his rage force his hand. He'd done it before with dire consequences, which was undoubtedly why his relationships with his father and majority of his siblings were so strained—not that many people were aware of that fact.

A passive-aggressive child, Kronus had grown to become a volatile teen, and later an icy giant devoid of all emotion in the hopes that closed-off nature ensured he wouldn't lash out ever again. Because of that cold-heartedness, he'd spent a long time caring for nothing but his own comfort, entertainment, and privacy—hence why he'd taken an entire island off the coast of England as his own private fortress after Invasion Day. The spoiled Prince of Thrakor hadn't cared for company or friendships, only solitude and time to enjoy the peace he'd craved his entire existence. Only his personal guard and most trusted servants were allowed onto the island previously known as Jersey, but that was now referred to a Kro Island, and he'd always intended to keep it that way.

"Get me a craft," he said into what anyone else would've assumed was the empty nothingness around him, but he knew his Master Protector, Domo was there, as always.

"Yes, sire," Domo answered, and he moved out from his spot in the shadows. He went to a small device that was docked by the wall, programmed in the request, and then stood to attention in wait of Kronus's next order.

The King said nothing. He simply came to a stop and stared out of his window at the otherwise uninhabited island around him. Despite trying to force his feelings aside, he felt something for the first time in his long life—emptiness. He'd finally told someone he cared, and had let himself allow that consideration for another to penetrate his rock-hard exterior for the first time since that night on the rooftop terrace. Kronus still couldn't believe he'd come across that same girl again, and had been stunned to discover that she'd made her way up the army ladder without ever using stories of their incredible experience to help further her career. Kyra had kept that secret the entire time, and for some reason it'd made him immensely proud of her. He guessed it was because he was an incredibly private person, and the knowledge that she could keep something like that to herself, rather than flaunt her story to anyone who wanted to hear it, was an endearing quality in anyone, especially in a woman. He'd never felt more attracted to someone in his entire life.

She truly was unlike any other woman he'd known, human or Thrakorian. Fresh anger bubbled up in him again when he remembered how Thrayke had described his new lover before he'd had the opportunity to meet her. He'd told Kronus how she was unusual, different to anyone he'd met before. He'd gone on and on about how beautiful, clever, kind, and funny she was, and at the time Kronus had simply nodded along, as if he even knew what it felt like to care for another so profoundly. What had shocked him though, was how Thrayke, the eternal bachelor, was evidently seriously second-guessing his aversion to having proper relationships because of the woman he'd spoken so fondly of. He had then come clean about the treatment he'd asked Greegis to give her, and its success, but it hadn't mattered to Kronus at the time. He'd had no reason to be concerned for her wellbeing. She was just another human, and another life he cared nothing for, while he remained stagnant and in limbo. Thrayke was his oldest friend, and at the time, Kronus had simply nodded and offered him his blessing.

However, when he'd spotted that cross shaped scar on her cheek, the unconquerable world he'd created for himself had instantly fallen apart. His initial shock had given way to anger, jealousy, denial, and then fear. If Kyra had been killed during her treatment he might never have found her again, and that thought alone was enough for him to issue the order that Thrayke not see her anymore. He couldn't believe Thrayke had been so careless, and he hated knowing his loyal soldier and friend had been so cavalier with the life of the one person Kronus felt somehow belonged to him. He didn't even feel guilty for ordering that he break things off with her, only bitter that he'd had the opportunity to be with Kyra before Kronus could steal her away to have her for himself.

But therein lay the other problem. He wasn't on Earth to take lovers. He most certainly wasn't there to find a purpose to life other than being a good and loyal subject of his father, King Thrakor. As was his father's wish, Kronus was betrothed to another—Mariah. When their mission was complete, he knew that he'd be expected to leave this planet behind, and that he'd be married within weeks of returning home. As part of his betrothal, and as was downright expected of him given his nobility, he'd remained pure and loyal to Mariah in readiness for their wedding, as would she have been for him. He'd never so much as touched another woman, and hadn't wanted to, until Kyra. Regardless of his desire for another though, the truth remained that he couldn't offer her a future. Kronus knew he would be a better man just letting Kyra and Thrayke be together, but he simply couldn't do it.

She was his, and part of him wished he'd kept her close ever since Invasion Day. He'd recently read her files and knew what a tough life Kyra had led since that day, and it pained him to think of how hard times had been for her. She would've made a superb companion for him to nurture and groom, rather than leaving her to grow up alone and unloved in the slums. But in doing so, she'd blossomed into an extraordinary woman with her own ideas and a voice that demanded to be heard. She'd never have reached her full potential beneath his iron-fisted upbringing. Even Kronus knew that. He was envious of everything she'd become without him, and how happy she'd been in spite of having nothing but her drive to keep her going all these years. Kronus cursed himself for all he'd failed to do by her, but also wondered if he'd even still want Kyra without that clever, headstrong mind of hers.

He thought how his soldiers had never seen him act tenderly towards another, or even associate with a human during his visits to Earth in the years before they'd invaded. Rumors had been aplenty following his arrival on Invasion Day, but he'd soon quashed them and then made sure to never show that side of himself again. Kronus had hardened, grown disinterested and less humane with every passing year, and wished he'd known how to deal with the almost instant demolition of those walls when happenstance had brought Kyra Millan back to him.

"How long?" he barked, having realized a good few minutes had passed while he was deep in thought, and he turned to find his men all waiting patiently for him in the doorway. They were stood to attention, dressed in their black combats, and geared up—ready for any action that might come their way.

"We didn't want to disturb you," Domo said, and he tossed Kronus his armored jacket. His Master Protector was incredibly wise, but also very opinionated, even if he didn't actually say much. By leaving his leader alone with his thoughts, Domo had let Kronus internally analyze all the things he didn't want to say aloud. None would dare try to make him see sense or learn his lessons, but he could certainly beat himself up aplenty when left alone with his thoughts, and that was often how Domo chose to teach his young King the error of his ways. The two men of very few words worked well together, until matters of the heart had eaten the unlikely one of them alive, and only then had the King come to realize just how much he relied on the faithful service of those he'd brought to Earth with him. "New Delhi?" Domo asked, and his deep grey eyes shone despite the darkness.

"New Delhi," Kronus agreed, and the group set off for the loading dock at the rear of the huge house. None of them said a word, and while he appreciated it, Kronus suddenly hated the silence. It made his mind wander. He went over the information Thrayke had relayed again, and tried to make sense of the knowledge that Kyra had disobeyed his orders and stayed in the city with the rebel scumbag, Tuka. Her fellow treacherous comrade, Gage, was back at the holding facility, but reportedly hadn't been able to offer much more than an apology, and an assurance that she hadn't betrayed them and turned rebel herself. By all accounts, Kyra had refused to come back based on her instincts that they were onto something with Tuka and his gang. Reportedly, they weren't ordinary rebels interested in fighting the Thraks for their freedom, but a team of specialized recruits working toward another goal. She'd joined them and earned their trust to discover what that goal was, and Kronus had to believe that she would come back when she was ready, or else he was more than willing to go after her himself if he had to.

"We've had a team watching the house in which General Gage was with Tuka and General Millan. We've also had the underground brothel under surveillance, but both are quiet—seemingly empty," Thrayke immediately began informing Kronus as he disembarked his craft. He carried on with his update as they walked down the long hallway toward the interrogation room, where Gage awaited the pair of powerful men.

Being back there made Kronus remember the last words he'd said to Kyra, and he wished she was holding onto them now. There was an old saying about letting something you loved go knocking around in his mind, and if this was what that meant, he decided he officially hated humans and their stupid sayings.

"Where might they have gone? Did she give you anything you could go on?" Kronus didn't even introduce himself to Gage, he simply dived right into his questioning, and then paced the small space in front of the timid man.

"She...she told me about her treatment. There are so many stories about testing going on around the world where humans are the test-subjects, and she had to know if they were true. She's still undercover, but I'm scared her genuine desire for the truth has taken her beyond just the role she was playing," Gage answered, and he almost jumped out of his seat when Kronus slammed his hands down on the table in front of him with a loud bang.

"Are you saying she's gone rogue?" he demanded with a growl, and knew it was coming out like a threat, but didn't care. There was no way she would betray him, not after everything she'd done over the years to serve his regime and earn her place in his human army. No chance at all she'd fall into the arms of the enemy rather than him.

"No, but I think she's lost her way. Something has made her doubt everything she thought she ever knew, and I fear she's looking to the wrong people for the answer," Gage answered, and then he looked from Kronus to Thrayke with suspicion in his eyes. "What was said to her before we left? Something made the light leave her eyes. Kyra's passion and drive was gone, and only her uncertainty remained. It seemed as if her entire world had turned on its head and she didn't know how to right it again."

Kronus knew exactly what'd made her doubt everything—him. He'd been so up and down he'd probably given her whiplash, and on top of that he'd then played the dumb alpha-male card and made Kyra think he'd actually let her live the rest of her life locked away and alone, rather than happy and fulfilled. He'd driven her away with his selfish outbursts, and knew he deserved to feel the ache currently radiating from deep within his gut. Kronus had never felt the powerful emotion before in his entire life, but knew right away what it was. Guilt was bubbling up inside of him, and he knew he'd never rest until he made things right.

"Get back to the control center and help them trawl through the photos and surveillance footage.

Hopefully we'll find something that might help us find her," he told Gage. He was back to talking in that same forced, flat tone he'd maintained ever since being informed of Kyra's deviation from their covert operation, and was surprised he was able to keep his cool. However, Kronus was glad when Thrayke took the boy back to the control room and he was left alone, because less than a second after the door closed, his anger overwhelmed him and he trashed everything he could get his hands on.

***

"Can you tell me what happened to your son, if you don't mind?" Kyra asked the small old lady sat before her, and she wrapped an arm around her timid guest when she started to cry. Weeks had now passed since she'd walked away with Tuka instead of Gage, and she'd heard so many stories her shoulders were more burdened than less. She'd hoped that in learning more it'd make it easier to understand, or to help her figure out what Kronus and his people were doing, but instead she felt more lost than ever.

Tuka had taken her under his wing, and had taught her to see the world without her previous rose-tinted glasses. Kyra was one of them now. Her opinions mattered, and she was emotionally stronger and more defiant than she'd ever been before. She sometimes felt like a phoenix—a far superior version of her former self that'd crumbled, but was then rebuilt from the ashes of her despair, and reborn with strength anew. No one messed with her, but at the same time, those who were scared and afraid to tell their stories to the others were opening up at last because of her gentle, empathetic nature. Kyra had already filled numerous books with her scribbled notes of stories and experiences as told to her by the civilians Tuka had taken her to meet, and she knew all she could do for now was wake up and start all over again day after day, but that there wasn't anything else she'd rather be doing.

"He went to ask for work, and they offered him credits in return for some of his organs," the woman finally replied, and she sobbed a little more. "He gave up a kidney, part of his liver, his spleen, appendix, and even a testicle. Eventually, he was incapable of giving any more, and he never came back. I know they killed him, they had to!" she cried, and looked absolutely ashen at the thought of having lost her child.

"Did he say anything the final day you saw him?" Kyra asked, urging her along, but she maintained her apathy toward the woman and her pain.

"He said he'd offered everything he had left and that it would be enough to keep us with a roof over our heads. He never returned, but I later received confirmation that my housing credits had been paid up until I die. He did it willingly so that I could live, but this is no life."

"No, it isn't. Thank you," Kyra replied, and gave the woman a squeeze before handing her a basket of various foodstuffs in thanks for sharing her story.

"How does it make you feel, all of this pain and suffering around you?" Tuka asked later when she joined him by the small fire they'd made to keep warm by in their temporary desert home.

"No better than I felt before, and I hate it. How can we still be no closer to figuring it out?" she asked, and let him wrap a protective arm around her shoulders, but didn't lean into his embrace. Kyra warmed her hands by the flames, and looked down at the scars on her arms. After forcing herself not to think about the man who'd both given and taken from her the night she'd gotten those scars, she was suddenly bombarded with images of him pulling her into his arms and peering down into her eyes. A smile curled at her lips when she thought of him, but she didn't let Tuka see. The rare smile wasn't for him, nor did she want to explain it to him. Kyra realized she missed Kronus, not the real version, but the one she used to fantasize about, and she hated that she'd lost the dream she'd once held so dear.

"Let me help make it better," Tuka said, and he grabbed her chin before turning her face to meet his. He leaned in for a kiss, but she pulled away, just like she had every other time he'd tried.

"It's not going to happen. How many times do I have to fend you off?" she replied, but smiled at his advance. He'd tried it on with her so many times now it was becoming a joke, but one they both seemed to be able to laugh about, and he shrugged.

"About another hundred, give or take," he said, and then turned his attention back to the fire. Together they sat watching the flames crackle and the wood burn in silence, and Kyra was glad. She didn't feel much like chatting.

Kyra fell into a deep sleep not long later, safe in her tent with some of the other women, but soon her dreams were haunted with the faces of those she hadn't seen in weeks. Even Tanner came to her, pleading for her to come home safely, and when the early dawn light woke her, it was a relief. In her dreams, she couldn't fight the fretful guilt brought upon her by so many faces that loved and cared for her—the faces of those she'd failed by not getting any further in her quest.

She needed to work harder, and push herself more. There was nothing else for it. Kyra knew she had to go deeper into her cover, even if she had to lose more of her real self in the process.

***

A few weeks' later, Tuka woke Kyra early. He threw a set of desert combats at her and a headscarf, informing her how she was to put them on and then meet him outside their camp ten minutes later. She did as he'd asked, and then headed over to rendezvous with her strange host, where she discovered Tuka leaning against a dune buggy with a cocky grin.

"Fancy a ride?" he asked, and Kyra knew it wasn't really a request, so hopped in. She wrapped the scarf over her face to make sure the dust didn't choke her, secured her belt, and then gave Tuka a thumbs up.

"Let's go!" she bellowed over the roar as he revved the engine to life, and they were off in a heartbeat. Kyra had to admit, the ride across the sand dunes was an exhilarating one, and she shrieked delightedly as he tore his way across the vast, empty desert with seemingly no real destination in mind.

When they came upon a deep valley, he pulled the buggy to a stop at the rim. Signs warning of contamination and radiation were dotted all along the entryways to the ravine, and Kyra watched Tuka thoughtfully. Was he going to continue on, regardless of the risks? She had to wonder, but hoped he wasn't planning on doing anything foolish. She'd been taught her entire life never to venture into the arid lands in the southern hemisphere. They'd been told that the areas had been blasted and polluted beyond repair during Invasion Day and then again many times since when the armies had tested weapons in the inhospitable areas. There was no way she fancied a walk around any the ruins of old that might lie beyond, and Kyra certainly hoped Tuka didn't think she'd find their discovery romantic or inspiring.

"Do you know what this place is?" he asked her,

and Kyra couldn't ignore the sadness in his tone, or deny that it had her intrigued. She shook her head no, and he peered out at the valley, deep in thought.

"Is it one of the mass graves you found?" she tried, but Tuka told her no.

"Not of the innocent, they're killed in labs like rats and then dumped once they're no longer of any use. This place is one of their hunting ranges. They bring convicts and rebels here, set them free, and then hunt them down for the fun of it. Those damn aliens think nothing of killing our kind for sport." Kyra took a look down into the crater-like ravine, and quickly realized that Tuka wasn't lying. She could see for herself how there weren't any roads that accessed the bottom. It was clear that the only way inside was to either drive over the edge and into the ravine with no hope of getting back out, or to transport down using a craft. It made sense that it could be a Thrak-made course full of tunnels and mazes in which the prey could hide and the predators could hunt, and Kyra shuddered.

"Have you seen them?" she had to ask. A glutton for punishment, she needed to know more. Tuka nodded, and then rubbed his bald head forlornly.

"Yeah. One of our guys was captured and brought here. We followed them via his chip's signal, remember how I told you we had a way of hacking the microchips?" Kyra nodded. "Well, this was before they found a way to catch us hacking them. My guy was running up and down in just this one area, and we thought at first it could be a glitch, but then we reached the summit here and caught the show for ourselves."

"Caught the show? As in, they'd made an event out of it?" Tuka gave her a slight nod, and Kyra was gob-smacked. She'd heard of their hunting for sport, but hadn't ever figured that the Thrakorian's might actually have set up events with an audience for their gruesome hunting arena.

"Rows and rows of ships were here to watch as they brought out teams of five or six humans at a time and gave them a five-minute head start. They weren't given any form of weapon or guidance, only told to make a run for it. The Thraks loved it when some either tried to hide or escape up the banks here," he told her, pointing down to the steep edges of the ravine that Kyra knew would be impossible to scale. "They teased and tormented them, ignoring their pleas for mercy, before…"

Kyra didn't want to hear any more. She kept her expression solemn, but her heart bled for the victims sacrificed for the Thrakorians' entertainment. Deep down, she knew she ought to be angry at the likes of Kronus and Thrayke whether they'd been involved in it or not, however she pushed all of her real emotion away and focused instead of maintaining her cover. Here and now, she wasn't Kyra Millan. She was Kiki Paynter, and rather than keep a cool head like she'd been taught to during her army training, she let herself tremble as though disturbed by the terrible events that'd reportedly happened on the land stretching out before her.

Kyra knew that any other ordinary civilian human would find what Tuka had just told her so frightening they might cry or break down if they were weak enough, but she'd painted Kiki as a timid yet determined young woman, so let her eyes well up but not tear. Their stories were tragic, just like all the others, but she stood taller and simply looked across into Tuka's piercing blue eyes with steely resolve.

"I'll add this tragedy to the accounts already taken, Tuka. I'll make sure these victims aren't forgotten." He let out the breath he'd been holding and turned to her with adoration in his gaze.

"I knew I'd made the right choice with you,

Kiki. You see this world through such wise eyes, and I know you've seen more than you let on. I'd like to hope that one day you'll open up and let me in, because I know you've undoubtedly got an amazing story to tell."

"When the time comes and I'm ready to open up, you'll be the first one I come to. I promise," she lied, and yet Tuka didn't seem to notice her insincerity at all. In fact, he seemed even more besotted with Kiki Paynter than ever.

CHAPTER EIGHT

Over time, Tuka got pushier with his advances, and Kyra knew she was at a 'do or die' point in her relationship with the rebel mastermind. Their tight-knit group didn't go along to the few gatherings following her inclusion in their ranks, and she often wondered if it was perhaps that he was afraid her fake husband might gatecrash the event and take her away from him.

After having spent months together, she'd filled another huge pile of notebooks with stories, and it was then that Tuka finally got the call from above saying they were expected to attend the next meeting of initiates in Istanbul, Turkey. Kyra went along with him, and was filled with wonder at how modern and crowded the ancient city was. Once a renowned tourist resort, it was now a bustling metropolis of skyscrapers and other buildings dedicated to the business sector. At first, she thought they couldn't possibly be in the right place for a gathering, but she soon saw for herself the civilian homes dotted along the coastline just outside of the city and knew the residents were the target audience for their rousing recruitment drive. One such house was to be their residence for the few days they'd be in Turkey, and Tuka took great pleasure in showing her around.

"We're sharing this time, my dear," he said, indicating to the few bedrooms and overly crowded house. He'd come with his full team, and she'd thought it odd that he'd decided to bring them all along—until now.

"I'll warn you, I snore," she replied playfully, and then threw her bag inside onto the huge bed.

Tuka had hold of her in an instant, and he grabbed Kyra's chin in his powerful hands. He pressed his forehead against hers, and stared into her eyes menacingly. There were no games to be played or harmless banter that could deter him now, and she knew their period as mere companions was over. It was clearly time to pay her debts.

"No more games, no more teasing. You're mine now, and it's time you showed me how grateful you are for my hospitality," he warned, sneering at her before planting a harsh kiss against her lips. Kyra stood as tall as she could, and kissed Tuka back just as hard. She wasn't about to let him intimidate her. There was no emotion in her kiss, or even a hint of desire, but she was willing to carry on pretending for as long as it took to find a way in with the rebel leaders they'd be meeting with later that evening. She wasn't about to back down now that she was so close, and decided if she did have to give herself to him, it'd be on her terms.

"Don't treat me like just another one of your silly girls, because we both know I'm as big of a shark as you are, and just as ferocious," she replied, and planted another kiss on his lips, softer this time. "If I tell you no, that means no. I'm here on my own accord, and I won't be pressured into anything—by you or anyone else." That got his attention, and thankfully Tuka took it as a challenge rather than a refusal.

"You're massively different from all those other girls, Kiki. That's why I've allowed these games to continue between us for so long. I find myself hypnotized by you. Fascinated. I want you so badly I can't think straight—"

"You'll have me when you stop playing games, and when you're ready to show me how much you appreciate my company. Not the other way around. When I get what I want, you'll get what you want," she added with a smoldering stare into his deep blue eyes.

Kyra then sauntered away without so much as a backwards glance, and was surprised when he didn't come after her. She knew she'd gotten away with it this time, but also that his patience wouldn't last long, and so made sure she stayed nestled amongst the men and women already settling down to dinner below them for the rest of the afternoon.

Tuka eventually came down, took his seat beside her, and gave Kyra a wink.

"After the meeting tonight I'll show you just how much I appreciate you, Kiki," he said, and she grinned back at him. She didn't know if he meant it, but he seemed ready to give her the upper hand at last, and she enjoyed the feeling of satisfaction it gave her.

"I'm looking forward to it."

"Good, and in that case you won't mind staying behind," he said, and her smile quickly turned into a scowl. "It has come to my attention that your husband's in town, so I think it'll be best for you two to stay separated. I wouldn't want you getting confused about your feelings."

"I won't. Timmy knows I left him behind, and that I did it for you. He wants to join our cause, just like before. You should invite him back here after the gathering," she tried, but it was no use. Tuka clearly wasn't budging. She wanted to curse, but forced herself to remain stoic.

"I'll believe it when I see it," he answered, and then took Kyra's hand and led her from the table. She knew she had no choice but to follow, and when Tuka locked her in the bedroom, she didn't scream or shout out in defiance. Instead, she began plotting how she might evade his attention when he returned, because even contemplating being with him was suddenly turning her stomach. She knew the time had come to drop her façade and head back to reality, but she didn't know how—or if—she could. She'd enjoyed switching Kyra off and being Kiki for a while, but not any longer. Kiki had a dangerous ally intent on making her more than just a friend; whereas Kyra had two men she wanted in her life but were out of reach both physically and emotionally. She felt more lost than ever and wasn't entirely sure which persona had the better end of the deal.

Kyra heard the group leave for the gathering a short while later, and knew better than to try the door. There'd undoubtedly be guards posted on the other side of it, and they would absolutely report any suspicious behavior from her back to their leader. They had no allegiance to her, and she knew it. Silence descended, as did the dim twilight and cool night air, and she tried to relax, but it was no use. Everything inside was suddenly screaming for her to run, and Kyra decided to read through some of her notebooks in a bid to take her mind off the night she guessed would be ahead of her when Tuka finally returned.

There were so many stories in the books that she'd started to forget them all. They seemed to be blurring together in one awful anthology of the pain and misery that'd been forced on her race by the beings they'd been trained to serve. Each story was either about an abduction, loss of an organ, or worse—a child. Her heart had broken every time a man or woman had talked to her about their loss, and reading them back made tears well in her eyes.

She heard a small thud from outside the doorway, and checked her watch. It wasn't time for Tuka to be back already, and she sat absolutely still while desperately trying to listen in on a conversation, or even better, a disagreement that could potentially be going on outside that might give her the distraction she needed to make her escape. Anything would do, and Kyra would then slip away into the darkness and never look back.

There was nothing but the sound of the crickets outside and the hum of the city in the distance, though. She figured perhaps she'd been mistaken, or that she'd been so hopeful for a chance of escape that any noise had left her eager for her shot at freedom. Kyra was about get back to her reading when the door to her room was kicked in from the other side. It burst open with such force she had to shield her eyes from the splintered shards of wood that cascaded down around her.

When she looked back up, she couldn't believe her eyes, and shot to her feet. There, dressed all in black, and covered in black camouflage makeup, stood Thrayke. The whites of his eyes were the only part of his body that pierced the darkness and bore into hers, and Kyra's knees went weak beneath her. She swayed, and at first was grateful when he caught her, but then started fighting his hold, trying to pull away.

"Kyra, please. You need to come with me now!" he implored her, and she shook her head. She was suddenly confused. Her name was Kiki and she was a rebel, not someone who went off into the night with Thrakorian soldiers. Tuka's face appeared in her minds eye, but instead of being filled with loyalty towards him and his cause, she felt afraid. Kyra knew that if she stayed she would have to give herself to him, and that deep down, she wasn't able to go through with it.

Thrayke sensed her confusion, and shrugged. "I don't have time to convince you. I'm sorry," he informed her, and then threw her over his shoulder. She felt like she were two people living in one body, the rebel and the soldier, and both wanted two very different things. She kicked and fought, but all the while she was also so grateful that he'd come for her she wanted to kiss him. Thrayke cursed and muttered something about her being a pain in the ass, but she didn't care.

They were downstairs and out into the street in a second, where he threw her into the back of a truck and they sped away. Something inside of her then went feral, and she lunged at Thrayke. The driver swerved as he attempted to avoid her flailing limbs, but it was Thrayke who was being pummeled with punches and kicks, and he eventually had to hold Kyra down by force. He pinned her to the seat, flipped her over onto her stomach, and then captured her wrists behind the small of her back. Kyra couldn't move, and cursed loudly before having no other choice than to calm down and remain still in his unyielding grip.

"You'll never make it out of here with me as your captive. Tuka has his soldiers posted everywhere," she mumbled, while her ex-lover pressed her cheek into the dark leather.

"We've taken out the team watching over you, so he won't know you've gone until it's already too late. You were one of the last jobs on the to-do list. And don't worry, we aren't trying to get you out of the city yet, just away from that scumbag and into a holding cell where you can calm down. You might not realize it now, but I'm the best damn thing that ever happened to you, Kyra," he informed her matter-of-factly.

She went limp, and he seemed to sense that her fight had gone—for now at least—and let his hold loosen a little. Kyra turned her face to look at him, and immediately started sobbing into the seat. Thrayke released his hold, grabbed her, and pulled her up into his arms, shushing her and stroking her hair with the same delicate strength she'd once known so very well.

"Why did you save me? How?" questions were

coming out of her thick and fast, and while he knew exactly why she had to know, for some reason he refused to answer her. "I don't know who I am anymore, or what life I'm living. I just…don't know…"

"Your name's Kyra Millan. You were born and raised in Los Angeles," Thrayke started telling her a life story of someone she knew long ago, and while she didn't want to listen, she couldn't help but hear his words as they reverberated through her. "You're a General in the Human Royal Armed Forces, and one of the Intelligence Division's Gentry officers. You're a geek and you love relics from the old world. You adore anything that connects you to a past you also wish you could forget, because you're a weirdo who likes to punish herself rather than others."

"The things your people have done…I'm ashamed to know you—to want you," she groaned against him, sensing her rage returning, but Thrayke only held her tighter. He didn't respond or explain their reasons why, nor did he ask her why she was saying such things.

In a moment of clarity, Kyra guessed that he was simply there to support and help her transition out of her undercover persona and back to herself. He'd undoubtedly return to forcing her back at arms length again in no time at all, so she savored the feeling of having his arms wrapped around her, thinking that it might just be the last time.

"Your name's Kyra Millan," Thrayke began again, and he repeated the words over and over as they sped away. She felt lost and confused, like a child in Thrayke's embrace, and suddenly smaller than ever before.

Her head felt fuzzy, and before long she zoned out, and a vision of another huge Thrakorian came to the forefront of her mind. He also said a few lines to her over and over, but they were different to Thrayke's.

I'm sorry, Kyra. I'm so sorry.

She didn't realize that they'd stopped, or when she was out in the cool night air again in Thrayke's arms. As though drunk and clinging to a lucid dream, all she could focus on was her vision. He was the ghost that'd haunted her regardless of the mission, and a hallucination that felt so real it terrified her. He was holding his hand out, pleading with her to take it, but instead of going to him, she cowered away, back into the arms of her rescuer.

The sad apparition of King Kronus turned away, seemingly ashamed of her response, and she shuddered, but held on tighter to Thrayke. She felt as if he was the only thing keeping her grounded, and Kyra let him carry her inside. Only then did it dawn on her that what she'd seen was no vision at all, but very real, and how she'd hurt him by cowering away.

"Kronus?" she whispered, and the disheartened man's face reappeared. He looked down at her with hope in his gaze, but his shoulders sagged with the many burdens he was clearly carrying on them. He looked different, slimmer and more sullen, and he had a thick dark beard that now dominated his once so chiseled features. There was no light in his eyes, but the kindness still resonating within them gave him away, and she watched him while being carried by the now silent Besieger. They went into a dim and dismal building somewhere she assumed must be in the business sector of the city, and inside were a team of Thrakorian soldiers all standing to attention in wait for their leader's next command. "Kronus?" she asked again when they came to a stop, and heard the gasp some of his men took at her informal use of his name.

"Yes, Kyra?" he answered, but she said nothing more. She'd simply had to check that he was really there, and not a dream like she'd first thought.

Curled in a ball against Thrayke's muscular body, she watched as the stone walls of the building around them turned to metal, and then they were in a cage. It took her a moment to realize they were in an elevator, and by the time it stopped, she was finally beginning to unclench her white knuckles from the lapels of Thrayke's black shirt. He came to a stop and gently lowered her onto a bed, but waited until she let go before he took a step back.

"Thank you," she managed to tell him before he was part of the shadows again, and she was left alone with the bearded form of the man she'd been conditioned to both love and hate through her mixed up new life.

"I want to be angry with you, but I can't be. I did this. I pushed you away, and I'm so sorry," Kronus mumbled, staring down at her forlornly. She looked up and knew he was telling her the truth, but rage was building inside of her again, and she started wringing her hands in a bid to stop herself from lashing out at him.

"I need you to leave me alone. I can't deal with this right now, please just go," she pleaded, but Kronus didn't move a muscle.

"I'm a spoiled, foolish and elitist child, Kyra. I've been a selfish coward all my life, except the one time a little girl was crying in a rose bush and I decided to help her. I should've kept you safe even after then, but instead I chose to let you go without ever learning your name or asking them where they sent you."

"Stop, please," she begged, and began clutching at her aching gut.

"And then one day, just another day in the life of this egocentric and arrogant asshole, you walked back into my life with no warning at all. I took one look at that scar on your cheek and knew fate had brought you back to me, but instead of taking care of you, I did it again. I sent you away, just like before, however now I know it's because I was terrified of how you make me feel. You make me crazy, Kyra, but being without you makes me even crazier."

She lunged at him, like she had in the car with Thrayke, and her fists flew like a woman possessed. She clawed and gouged, punched and slapped him, but nothing was easing the pain within. Tears rolled down Kyra's face, and her anger consumed her, but Kronus just let her hurt him in whatever way she wanted. He didn't fight back. He simply stood there and took the best beating she could muster, and only when her muscles gave out did she finally fall back onto the bed in defeat.

"How many people have you killed? How many have you tested on? Hundreds? Thousands?" she asked, holding the stitch in her side while he took a seat next to her on the bed.

"Try millions," he answered, and put his head in his hands.

"Why?" she breathed.

"Because we need you, the humans that is. Our race has developed an autoimmune disease called Ehrad. We cannot cure it, and we need to find an answer in our DNA as to why." He looked back up at her with bloodshot eyes that showed forcefully unshed tears, but screamed with the agony within. "Your race holds the answer."

"So you kidnap entire families and murder them in the name of science?" she yelled with renewed strength, but then fell back again as tears fell anew. "And babies? You take them, too?"

"Yes." At least he was being honest, she had to give him that, but it didn't make any of this easier.

"And do what?" she demanded. "What use are they to your research?"

"We crack the genetic code and look for a match we can reconstitute it with. Combining the chromosomes helps force the human DNA to evolve like ours. It's all research at the moment in a bid to find a new sequence that works and we hope that what we find can eventually be used to help my race advance further."

"Like with me?"

"Like with you," he concurred.

Kyra felt like she might be sick, and slid off the bed onto the cold floor in a heap. She felt his strong arms scoop her up off the ground, and didn't fight when Kronus lifted her into his lap and held her close. He wrapped his arms around her, holding her still. He'd never held her this way, and while it felt odd, she didn't fight it. Kronus then climbed back, placing her beside him on the bed. He watched her, but she couldn't meet his gaze. Kyra still had more questions.

"Then why didn't they kill me and dissect me like all the others?"

"Because your sequence was a failure. The computer program that decodes the DNA sequences rejected your new code. It happens in over ninety percent of the people we've tested."

"And then what usually happens to people like me?" she hated asking, but had to know the truth, even if it killed her to finally learn it.

"They're normally dug a shallow grave and never seen again, rather than let them live with their new gifts. You were saved only because of Thrayke and his affection for you." Tears came thick and fast, and Kyra didn't try to fight them. She knew for sure now how she'd really had no clue what she'd gotten herself into back then, and felt more lost than ever now that she knew how and why things had turned out the way they had. Out of the many that'd been given the treatment, Kyra was the one and only lucky test subject allowed to live, and yet she felt far from lucky to have survived Greegis and his team of scientists. If anything, she felt cursed.

CHAPTER NINE

Kyra stirred the next morning to the strange feeling of roughness against her temple, and she wondered for a minute what it was. She opened her eyes and smiled. As she gently stroked the thick beard she was still trying to get used to on Kronus's face, she sighed. No matter what awful lessons she'd learned, the instinct to love and worship her savior was still ever-present, and watching him sleep was a treat she hadn't counted on enjoying before that morning.

She remembered her teachings about him and his race as a child, and how those alongside her in the foster homes and schools who'd struggled to accept the Thrakorian rule weren't punished for their slow progression right away. At the time, it'd seemed like a kind gesture to her tiny mind, but she'd later found out how the offenders were given a specialized form of detention, and one not everybody knew about. In those private sessions specializing in behavior control, the children had reportedly been converted using a variety of propaganda driven messages and scare tactics. One of her friends had told her afterwards how they'd been sat down and made to watch a video showcasing all the awful things the human race had done over the past few thousand years, and that it'd been a terrifying lesson in humility the six year old child had never forgotten. Kyra hadn't needed those intense sessions in the slightest. She'd put her trust in her rescuer that night on the rooftop and it'd never faltered, not even when he'd made a point of proving how much of an arrogant ass he could be.

Part of her wondered if she could ever truly love Kronus, or if she was in love with the fictional version she'd molded over time with her infatuation of a myth. It was a question she'd never seriously asked herself before, but having woken up wrapped in his arms, she felt like she could fall for his real persona—if only he could love her back.

And then there was the problem of the other part of her heart. It didn't belong to Kronus, but to the man who'd been her lover and mentor until he'd been ordered to break things off. Thrayke was at the forefront of her mind, regardless of whom she'd woken up beside, and she felt a smile curl at her lips when she thought back to their time together before Kronus had come back into her life and turned it upside down.

Despite his insistence that they would never be anything more than a casual affair, she missed Thrayke, and who they'd been for one another while together. Time might be the only way she could tell where her heart truly belonged or which half prevailed, and in the meantime, she figured she'd settle for them both being her friend. Kyra hoped with all her heart that the rollercoaster of a life she'd endured the past few years might just slow down enough to let her catch up, and then she might finally be able to start making the right choices with regards to her future.

A slight movement over by the door caught her eye, and she turned to find five huge Thrakorian soldiers stood to attention just a few feet away from the end of the bed by the elevator door. Their presence surprised her, but then again she knew it had to be expected with the King around, especially while away from his fortress home. Kyra sat up and smiled over at the men in greeting, but not a single one of them moved a muscle or addressed her in return. They were clearly the ultimate in elite agents who lived to protect their sovereign, and she guessed they'd probably stayed up all night to watch over him.

Despite the actually rather crowded room, not a sound reached her ears. It was eerie thinking how they'd all watched her sleep, and she blushed with embarrassment when she realized they must've also seen her fall apart the night before.

Kyra slid to the edge of the bed to stand and stretch, choosing to leave her shame behind and focus instead on the future ahead. There were no certainties when it came to what Kronus was or wasn't planning on offering her, but she promised herself she'd hear him out, and hoped they'd try and become something to one another, even if it was just friends.

As she watched the lineup deep in thought, looking at them but not seeing, she realized the man in the center of the group blocking the elevator doors was Thrayke. She immediately went to him and wrapped her arms around his waist, and was sure she heard the Thraks to each side gasp in shock at her actions. Kyra guessed no other human, female or not, had been so overly familiar with the Thrakorian noblemen before, but she didn't care for formality. Thrayke had to know how much she cared for and appreciated him.

Just like the others, his arms were linked behind his back by the wrist. Thrayke was standing at ease, and he was perfectly still—like a statue. He remained motionless at first, sticking to his professionally enforced stance, but then couldn't seem to help himself. Kyra felt his arms loosen just slightly as his heart and head seemed to be battling things out within him. When he sighed deeply, muttered a curse, and then wrapped his arms around her in return, she had to smile. No matter the distance between them, he was still ready to comfort her, and she was eternally grateful that he still wanted to after everything they'd been through.

Kyra held onto him so tight she thought he might pull away, but instead Thrayke just stayed there, giving her what she needed despite their audience. She knew it was selfish, but she craved as much affection as she could get, and was glad he seemed to understand that need. She took a deep breath, inhaling him. He smelled good—like sweat and boot polish—and it reminded Kyra of a life she missed more than she'd realized. Her heart and soul were in the army, not amongst the rebels, and there was no way she'd let herself forget her place ever again. She nestled against him some more, and Thrayke's black combat jacket was rough against her cheek, but she still didn't pull away. She was torn between whether to hold on longer, or pull away and let him go, but for the time being her heart was winning rather than her head.

Kyra suddenly felt like crying. She wondered if she let go, would it be for the last time? She wasn't sure she was ready for that yet, and guessed she might finally be mourning the relationship she'd lost and the connection between them she knew might never return.

"Are you okay?" his whispered voice found her ear, and she forced herself to nod.

"Thank you for saving me," she murmured into his chest where her head was still resting. "You're a good man, Thrayke. An amazing man. I don't want to say goodbye."

"Me neither," he whispered so quietly she knew the response was just for her. "And jeez woman, talk about denting my reputation as a badass," he then teased, and she giggled. Kyra was glad he'd chosen to lighten the mood, and hoped it was his way of coping too.

"Well, I guess you *were* pretty badass last night, all covert ops and stuff," she replied, and looked up into his face with a smile. He'd wiped away his camouflage makeup, but was still filthy and in need of a shower. The dark, oily cream made the lines of his face seem more pronounced, but he didn't look older because of them, only somehow more distinguished. "It was impressive, and incredibly cool. Did you even get any sleep?" she asked, having noticed the dark circles under his eyes that had nothing to do with the black cam-cream, and he shook his head.

"We've been standing guard over the two of you since we got here. Sleep is overrated anyway," he answered with plenty of obviously forced nonchalance, and Kyra felt her cheeks burn that he'd seen her at both her most vulnerable and volatile.

"So you saw what I did to him? Why didn't any of you stop me?"

"Because he ordered us not to intervene, no matter how you reacted. Even if you lashed out at him. I think he kind of deserved it, but don't tell him I said that." Kyra laughed quietly and shook her head.

"How can I compare anyone to you two after all of this?" she asked before she'd fully thought what she was opening up about, and he smiled down at her with nothing but affection in his intense gaze.

"Have we ruined you for all humankind? Perhaps it really is a matter of, 'once you go Thrak, you never go back...' or something like that," he mumbled with a cheeky grin. His silliness made her smile broader, but Kyra felt herself growing more confused, rather than surer of what she wanted. The fundamental facts remained though, and she knew that learning the truth was far more important than figuring out where her heart belonged.

"There was so much I didn't know before, so much I yearned to find out. And now I do know, I'm not sure I can process it all," she mused aloud, and then laid her head against his chest again. She realized that having been watched over by Thrayke and his team also meant they'd heard everything that'd been said between her and Kronus, and she hoped they would each keep their mouths closed about their history and her revelations.

Kyra didn't know how it worked in the Thrakorian army, but she knew many humans who would've loved having that sort of knowledge to use against the King. The immense amount of Thrakorian loyalty was hopefully worth more than that to them, and she hoped she was right to trust the noble race of men who surrounded her not to repeat or spread gossip about their odd love triangle.

A deep cough from behind alerted Kyra to the obvious fact that Kronus was awake, but she didn't care that he'd caught her and Thrayke having their moment of quiet resonance. The awareness that she was a small fish in a sea filled with sharks remained, and because of that lack of power she held, she couldn't be sure if or when she'd have an opportunity to thank Thrayke for everything he'd done for her again. She'd most likely be back in The Tower with a full work schedule as soon as she'd been fully rehabilitated again. It was a bittersweet prospect, but a future she knew she deserved. However, Kyra still felt she'd earned the chance to tell her friend and mentor exactly how much she appreciated him, regardless of their history as lovers.

"Is the transport ready?" Kronus then asked his men, and as Kyra turned and walked back toward the bed, she heard one of the soldiers answer from behind her.

"Yes, sire. A craft is on the roof at the ready."

"Excellent, let's go," he answered, and stood just as Kyra reached him. She wasn't sure what to say to him, or how to act after their intense conversation the night before, and she fumbled on the spot in wait for him to tell her what to do next. He didn't seem interested in addressing her awkwardness though, and Kronus reached down and cupped Kyra's cheek with his hand, pulling her gaze up to his. "We're taking you back home to The Tower, but I'll be staying for a while to help pull together everything we need to put an end to this rebel activity once and for all. Are you ready?" he asked, and let a smile curl at his lips that somehow also shone in his almost black eyes.

Kronus, the all-powerful leader of not only his own race, but also hers, mesmerized her. The softness he showed her seemed new to him, and while his features remained stoic, those eyes of his gave him away. He took her in as though memorizing her face, and Kyra felt her cheeks flush under his scrutiny. She eventually nodded, and smiled as he took her hand and led her back into the awaiting elevator.

They travelled up the few floors to the roof, and stepped straight out into the bright morning sunshine atop the vast building. Kyra took a deep breath of the fresh air. It was a glorious day, warm and without so much as a hint of a breeze. Silence seemed to have fallen over the city, but then all of a sudden, something didn't feel right. It was far too quiet.

"No chains to hold you prisoner, and no resistance to being led away by a pack of alien scum. Perhaps I really was wrong about you," Tuka's spiteful voice filled the silence, and Kyra looked across in time to watch him step out from behind the hovercraft they were about to board. The small squad of Thrakorian soldier's she was traveling with closed in around them, but she knew they were doing it to protect the King rather than her. Tuka clearly didn't care. He fixed her with a hard stare and carried on. "Almost my entire operation has been wiped out in one night by a squad of Thraks who stormed our gathering, and then when I returned home, I found you gone. Of course I feared the worst, especially after I discovered that your guards had been executed and the house was barely left standing. Naturally, I then spent the rest of the night tracking you down. I guess I needn't have worried after all, you treacherous bitch," he told her with a repulsive scowl.

Rebel soldiers then started pouring out of the stairwell exits and from behind the craft to join Tuka in his last stand, and Kyra recognized many of the faces there. She'd lived and worked alongside several of the men and women who'd come to be a part of his coup, and fear gripped her gut at how badly this would undoubtedly end for all of them. She didn't want Tuka's followers to get hurt, but at the same time, she was scared to her core for Kronus and his men. That same helpless feeling of confusing loyalty to both sides filled her head again, and in her confused state she realized she'd failed to notice the gun in Tuka's hand.

He lifted it, ignoring the Thrakorian soldiers and their leader. He seemed fixated on making her pay for having betrayed him, and he pointed the weapon directly at her head. In less than a second, the men and women he'd brought with him followed his lead, taking his action as a sign to initiate their fight, and they advanced on the handful of Thraks on the rooftop.

Battle commenced in a heartbeat, and rather than wilt under the precariousness of the situation, the soldier within took over. On instinct, Kyra assessed the situation, and she readied herself to fight, but strangely none of the rebels came at her. Her death seemed to be in the hands of one and only, and Tuka clearly wasn't letting anyone else have her but him. This was personal. Thrayke and the others started fending off their other attackers with apparent ease, but there were too many of them, and even Kronus joined in the fray, leaving her open to attack.

"Call this off and walk away, Tuka. You've already lost so much, don't let all these people die, too," she implored him, and didn't back away when he reached her and pressed the gun against her temple. "You know the misery I've had to live with, the pain I've had to endure via the stories those men and women told me in confidence. My apathy was real, my tears genuine, and if you kill me now they would've all suffered in vain. I'll fight for them from the inside, I promise."

"You made me many promises, Kiki. You made me believe in you and your word, and yet you broke them all. You betrayed our cause, and your race. How can I ever trust you again?" he demanded, but lowered the gun slightly, and she could see the pain in his eyes. It seemed the cold-hearted rebel really had cared for her after all, and Kyra hated how she'd broken another heart in her selfish pursuit for truth and a place in the world.

"Get away from him, Kyra. Get in the ship," Kronus's voice boomed from behind her, and Tuka's gaze finally shifted away from her face at the sound. He peered over her shoulder at the Thrak who'd spoken, and did a double take. Realization took over his features, and he open and closed his mouth in shock at who was standing in front of him.

"Don't do anything foolish," Kyra tried to tell Tuka, but knew it was no use. He was gone; his mind completely closed off to any order other than that to kill the dictator they'd been fighting for almost two decades. Anger surpassed the confusion on his face in a moment, and she knew exactly what he was planning to do. Tuka shoved her away from him, but his actions only managed to push her back in Kronus's direction, and when he raised his hand again, this time pointing the gun at their King, she acted fast.

Kyra turned on her heel and ran to Kronus. In

that moment, she knew with absolute certainty where her loyalty truly laid. There was no longer any doubt in her mind or heart. She was loyal to him and his reign, regardless of the wrongs done along the way, and she leapt up into the air as soon as she heard the weapon fire from behind her. Something heavy slammed into her back, knocking the wind out of her, and Kyra stumbled forward, reaching out to Kronus in a bid to reach him before more shots could be fired, but she couldn't seem to control her body.

She heard as Tuka bellowed out a curse at her for getting in his way, but then the sounds pouring from his mouth quickly changed from angry taunts to maniacal laughter. His mirth and provocation didn't matter though, as all Kyra could focus on was Kronus. Time slowed to a snail's pace as she watched his mouth move, bellowing orders she couldn't hear over the ringing in her ears. He was staring at her in shock and horror, and then ran to her, catching Kyra right before she could hit the ground in a crumpled heap.

Kronus cradled her in his arms, and she wondered for a moment why he looked so troubled, but then looked down and saw that dark-red blood was covering his shirt. He'd been sprayed with it, and she hated how sad he seemed. She tried to ask him whose blood it was, but choked on something hot and metallic that was lodged in her throat. Her chest burned and the world began to spin. Kyra coughed and wheezed, suddenly piecing together the gunshot with the pain that'd begun radiating from inside her ribcage, and she quickly realized the blood was hers. Tuka had shot her, but she didn't care. All she cared about was that she'd saved Kronus from taking the bullet, and she smiled.

Fear left her, and only peace remained as a wave of blissful darkness swept over her and pulled her under.

***

Kronus roared in torment as he watched the light fade from behind Kyra's eyes. This couldn't be happening. Not to him. For the first time in his long life he felt afraid, and he immediately grieved the tremendous loss of the life in his arms, as well as the future they might've potentially come to have alongside one another. She had to be dead. There was no way anyone could've survived a shot right through the chest like that, and Kronus cursed her for having taken it for him. Because of Kyra's actions, the bullet had torn through her body and given Kronus time to duck what would've undoubtedly been a shot through his heart—and instant death not even the most powerful of Thrakorian's could survive—but there was no triumph in her success. There was no gladness that she'd spared his life, only the pain and anguish in knowing she'd sacrificed her own to save him.

Down on one knee with Kyra's limp body curled against his chest, Kronus felt as though all that was good in the world was lost to him again, and only emptiness remained. He looked up and spotted Tuka fighting with one of his soldiers, and an injured one at that. It seemed he too had taken a bullet from the rebel scumbag in his attempt to assassinate their King, but now the gun had been kicked aside and he was unarmed. Kronus wanted Tuka for himself, and felt his lip curl into a sneer. It was finally time to unleash the beast he'd kept so carefully hidden away.

Someone put a hand on his shoulder from beside him, and he looked up to find a clearly grief-stricken Thrayke peering down at him. Despite the bright sunlight, a dark cloud was over his head as he took in the gory sight. He was mourning Kyra as fiercely as Kronus was—if not more so—and he too seemed ready to lay waste to all humanity in honor of her incredible sacrifice.

Feeling confused, Kronus couldn't remember if Thrayke had been beside him the entire time, or if he'd watched her get shot from further away, but he knew with absolute certainty that he had to be the one to do something about it. Vengeance would be his.

Kronus stood, handed the limp bundle of precious cargo over to Thrayke, and then ran at Tuka as fast as his huge legs could carry him. He bulldozed into him with the force of a wrecking ball, and starting pummeling the foolish man with punches to the face using fists over half the size of his head. Kronus didn't stop until Tuka was more than just dead, he was mush, and then he moved onto the next rebel, and the next. Like a man possessed, he took down one after another, leaving only a mess of broken bodies in his wake. Regardless of age, gender, whether they cried for mercy, or if their backs were turned, he took life after life in his quest for retribution. When he'd finally cleared the roof of all its invading rebel scum, Kronus actually felt disappointed that there weren't more for him to take his pain out on, and it took him a few moments to calm his frenzied breathing and see through his red-misted haze.

"She's gone, isn't she…" he asked, and could hardly bring himself to say the terrifying words. Kronus then fell down into the spot beside Thrayke on the ground with a thud. He took in the grisly sight before him, and took a tiny bit comfort when Thrayke shook his head no. There was still color in Kyra's cheeks, and he didn't know how, because her breathing had to be impossible with the hole currently taking residence in the center of her chest. She looked awful, but her brow wasn't furrowed, and neither did she seem afraid. Somehow, she actually looked peaceful. Kyra had known exactly what she was doing when she'd jumped in front of that bullet for him, and Kronus knew he'd never get the image of seeing the exit wound bust her chest wide open with the impact out of his mind as long as he lived.

"I think she's still alive, but I have no idea how. We need to get her to Greegis," Thrayke answered, and he stood, cradling Kyra's so tiny body in his arms, much the same way as he had the night before when he'd carried her up to the makeshift safe house. Kronus had to fight the urge to take her from him, but instead followed Thrayke's lead, and his men fell in line behind them.

Luckily, the pilot was uninjured, and he had them airborne in no time. Their small group were grateful to be heading away from the fray, but all any of them could seem to concentrate on was the somehow still beating heart of the heroic human woman lying in Thrayke's arms. If any of them had doubted her before, they'd most certainly been won over now, and each watched her with genuine concern etched on their usually so stoic faces.

"Where to?" the pilot called from the cockpit once they were up and nestled amongst the clouds, and Kronus reached out and took Kyra's hand in his. Against all odds, she was warm, and he sighed in sweet relief that perhaps he hadn't lost her after all.

He still couldn't believe she'd taken a bullet for him. What a myriad of surprises she was turning out to behold, and he knew he had to do the right thing by her as thanks. After everything she was still going though, and what he himself had put her through, she'd remained loyal to him and had risked her life to save his when it'd mattered. This incredible young woman had amazed him with every moment she'd spoken or acted in either defiance or devotion, and he knew she deserved so much better than how he'd acted towards her. Kyra was stronger than anyone he'd ever known, despite her being from the supposedly inferior race, and Kronus vowed he'd never underestimate her strength again.

She coughed and sputtered up more blood, but her eyes remained closed, and he hoped he might get to see those beautiful brown eyes of hers again before long. First, she had to heal, and he wanted to be by her side while she received the best care he could get her. It was evident there was no way he could save her the pain and suffering he knew was coming, but he would sure as hell try.

"Home. Take us to Kro Island," he shouted in response, and was just surprised by his reaction as any of them. He'd never let a human set foot there since clearing the island for his own personal use after Invasion Day, but now it was the only place he was sure Kyra would be safe, and he was finally willing to share it with her.

CHAPTER TEN

One minute, Kyra was floating in the clouds, and the next she was laying on a cold, hard floor. The darkness that'd first descended had given way to such lucid dreams that her visions almost felt real, and it was hard to follow her wayward thoughts as they scattered to the wind of her imagination, but then the strange back and forth started all over again. Her dreams were all over the place, and soon those same fretful nightmares she'd suffered during her treatment at the facility came back to haunt her. The faces of those she'd wronged or failed in the past came to mock and taunt her. The two rebels whose capture had been the pivotal moment in her career, and who were the reason she'd been promoted to Gentry, came and glowered at her. They spat in her face and laughed at her tears, growing taller and taller before eventually stamping her to mush. Her parents' rotting corpses also returned, and they told her again how she'd failed her race by betraying her humanity in return for a King's favor she would never truly have.

"Such a foolish little girl," her mother called her, before walking back into a mist that'd somehow swirled to existence around each of their ankles. Kyra then watched the horizon for a while, feeling lost and so alone that she even prayed for more company—friend or foe. Her dreams didn't relinquish their hold, or offer comfort, and suddenly she fell back onto the cold floor with a thud. Kronus and Thrayke then appeared, and the two men stood over her, each looking down at Kyra with pitiful stares.

"It's a shame, she was such a good little pet," Thrayke said in a clipped, emotionless voice, and Kronus agreed with a nod. "At least now we don't have to worry about letting her down gently. She can just die and leave us alone."

"Perfect scenario if you ask me," Kronus agreed, ignoring her tears. The pair of them taunted her a little longer, and then shook their heads, clearly disappointed that she wasn't strong enough to be with either of them after all. "We'll have to find someone new to play with, such a shame indeed," Kronus replied, and then the pair laughed loudly, mocking her.

"Can I have her back then? She'll be safe with me. I'll never let her out of my sight again," her overbearing ex-boyfriend, Silas, asked as he too appeared from the smoky abyss behind, and both Thraks nodded.

"She's no use to me now, you're welcome to her," Kronus answered a shrug, and they walked away while Silas scooped Kyra up off the ground and then flung her lifeless body over his shoulder. In an instant, they were back in Fort Angel, and he lowered her down onto the bed in his old room.

"I always said you belonged here with me. You should've stayed before when I asked you," he said, clicking his tongue and shaking his head, as though utterly displeased with her foolishness. She wanted to answer back, but somehow couldn't move or speak, and she started to panic. "Maybe I should punish you now, so I know you've learned your lesson and we can move on?" he asked, pretending she might answer, and then he slammed his hand down hard on her chest. The pain made her want to scream, but before she could react, he did it another time, and another. When Silas's apparition finally stopped his compressions, she was gone from the barrack room and adrift the clouds again, but the sun soon shone through, and for the first time what felt like forever, she took a deep breath.

***

"She's coming round," the sound of Thrayke's voice made Kyra open her eyes, but the pain in her chest made them roll back into her head again, seeking the comfort the oblivion brought with it. "No, don't do it again. The compressions worked, she's just going in and out of consciousness."

Kyra forced her eyes open again, and she eventually focused and saw Kronus standing at the end of the hospital bed she was now lying on. He had his arms wrapped around his chest protectively and was chewing on his thumb as though trying desperately to hold it together. When their eyes met, she tried to call his name, but nothing came out. Not even a hum or a croak left her lips. Kyra's voice was now nothing but empty air. Her hands flew to her chest, but were pulled away again by strong hands, and Thrayke's face came into her view, blocking Kronus out. "Don't touch it, we're getting you sewn up now. Stay still, otherwise you'll have to be sedated." Kyra tried to talk again, but there was still nothing, so she nodded.

She stared back down the bed at Kronus, and watched as he shifted his weight and gripped the bar at the end of the gurney she was laid on. His knuckles were turning white as he watched them working on her, and fear began bubbling up inside again. What was happening that'd made him so angry? Kyra was terrified that he might be mad at her for having jumped between him and Tuka's bullet, and she simply couldn't bear the look on his face as he regarded her. Perhaps the dream had been real after all and he was done with her? Kyra pleaded with Kronus to stop staring at her that way, but her words were still nothing more than silent pleas that never met his ears. The panic got the better of her, and she started trembling as her body went into shock. Hands gripped her from every angle, and Kronus cursed as he wrapped his hands around her ankles to hold them still.

Kyra wasn't sure why she was trembling so badly, she didn't even feel cold, but then she had trouble focusing on his face any longer. The bed was bouncing around beneath her, or so it seemed, and she frowned. Confusion turned back into agonizing torture in an instant when the realization hit that it was her juddering, not the bed, and her body quickly sent her mind back out of consciousness in a bid to find comfort in the depths of her psyche again.

It was silent when she came to again, and this time Kyra let herself lie there and listen to the sound of the ocean somewhere close by rather than rush to open her eyes. She wondered where they were, but found she didn't mind, and simply enjoyed the sounds of the Earth and its wildlife all around. Surprisingly, she felt pretty good, and wasn't sure if the pain had dulled, or if she was just high on painkillers. Kyra let her eyes flicker open, and she instantly wished she hadn't. She opened her mouth to scream, but no sound came out, and she couldn't be sure if it was still due to her injury, or thanks to the hand that was clasped over her mouth.

Lorde Greegis, the sadistic scientist from the facility she'd been administered her serum in, was standing over her. He leaned in closer, a little too close for Kyra's liking, but kept his hand firmly over her mouth in a clear bid to frighten her. His satisfied smile brought tears to her eyes, and she searched the room in the hopes she might find Kronus there watching over her again, but knew he would never allow such treatment if he were. They were alone, which was exactly what Greegis seemed to want.

"This is the second time my hard work and impressive scientific advancements have saved your life, so I suggest you think again before you try to outsmart me," he whispered in her ear. "Remember last time when I tested how quickly you could heal? I'd hate to have to show you again," he added, and she knew exactly what he was implying. When she'd stood up to him at the facility, he'd broken her wrist. While it'd hurt like mad, her new and improved body had healed the break within hours, and thusly hidden the evidence of his malpractice when Thrayke had come for her. Greegis was a scientist, not a doctor, but it was clear he hadn't liked being denied a test subject to study because of Thrayke's orders that she remain alive and whole at the end of her treatment, regardless of the outcome. She squirmed, but her body was still weak from her ordeal, and she knew fighting him was fruitless, so wilted.

While she was thankful for his serum and how it'd seemingly saved her from dying up on that rooftop, Kyra trembled and prayed to a God she hadn't believed in her entire life that he'd somehow meet a terrible end. She hated Lorde Greegis with a passion, and knew that hatred was also because of everything he and his fellow scientists had done in the name of progress. Millions of men, women, and children had lost their lives in his quest for whatever genetic jackpot the Thrakorian species seemed to be looking for, and he didn't care for the human losses one tiny bit.

The door opened, and by the time Kronus had come through it, Greegis had lowered his hand and was instead checking the pulse in her neck.

"How is she?" Kronus asked, and he came to a stop by the bed on her left side. She tried to talk to him, but no sound came out again, and he furrowed his brow at Greegis. Kronus sat down beside her on the bed, clearly just as distressed as he'd been the first time she'd awoken, and she had to fight the tears pricking at her eyes in knowing she was causing him such pain.

"Her larynx and vocal cords were badly damaged and are still healing. Her voice might come back, but it might not. Only time will tell," Greegis told him, and he then put a gentle hand on Kyra's shoulder. She hated how he could hide his monstrous side so easily in front of others, especially with how helpless she was to fight, and scowled back up at him. "Try not to talk, just let it come in its own time," he then added in his best impersonation of a caring doctor.

Kyra pulled away from Greegis and his fake care. There was no hiding her disgust, and she turned her body away from him and curled against Kronus. She didn't doubt that Greegis's threat had been a promise, and while she knew she had no other choice than to follow his demands and be a good little patient, she also knew she didn't have to play nice while doing it. He immediately backed off, and she heard his shoes scrape against the wooden floor as he backed away. "I'll check in with her in an hour," he offered, but Kronus shook his head.

"I'll take it from here. If I need you again I'll send for you," he replied, and Kyra was so glad he'd seemingly picked up on her fear of having the sinister man around longer than necessary. "Domo, see the good Lorde out."

The shock on his face was a victory, and Kronus's words struck the scientist dumb as he tried to fathom a way he might try and defy the King's order to leave. There was nothing he could reply with that wasn't tantamount to treason, and Kyra had to smile that he'd gotten at least a little bit of a comeuppance. She recognized the Master Protector who then stepped inside the doorway and shook Greegis's hand with what seemed to her like a forced smile.

"Thank you for your assistance, Lorde Greegis. We'll be sure to compensate you for the time spent away from your clinic. Please, follow me," he told him, and then led the way outside without another word. She could hear Greegis pleading his case as the door was closed behind him, but was glad to overhear that the soldier wasn't having any of it.

"I'm sorry, but we had to call him in. He created the serum you were given before, so was the only one we could trust to ensure you were treated properly this time," Kronus told her, and Kyra slowly started to unfurl her body from around his. She nodded, and hated that she couldn't talk to him about how she felt regarding Greegis, but was glad she was feeling better overall. Love him or hate him, thanks to Greegis and his serum she was alive and mostly intact, which was impressive considering she'd not long before jumped in front of a speeding bullet.

Kyra sat up and crossed her legs beneath her. She took a moment to clear her mind and untied the hospital gown from behind her neck, and then slowly pulled it down her arms so she could assess the wounds. There was no getting away from what'd happened, or putting off dealing with it any longer, and the first step was to finally see the damage for herself. Thankfully, someone had left her with her underwear on, but when Kyra looked down at her stitched up chest, the last thing she cared about was whether or not her body was on show.

A huge red scar went from her throat all the way to the base of her breasts, and the mottled skin was sewn together with thick, dark, surgical stitches. She shuffled to the edge of the bed and tested her weight on her feet, but Kronus was right there with her, and he put a gentle hand around her waist to keep her upright if she needed it. Kyra was standing strong a few seconds later, and while she felt tough enough to hold herself up without his help, she didn't push his hand away from the small of her back. It felt good, regardless of their situation.

Together they walked slowly across the room towards the mirror, and when she saw the wound reflected back at her in all its awful glory, she sobbed silently, and tears fell down her cheeks onto her sore chest. "It'll heal more, you just have to give it time," Kronus insisted, drying her eyes with the sleeve of his shirt. "Your body's already doing an amazing job. Let it finish before you get too disheartened."

How long has it been? she mouthed, and watched in the reflection as Kronus tucked a strand of her dark brown hair behind her ear. His eyes were on her neck, and he looked like he might kiss her, but then clearly thought better of it. Kyra didn't blame him, and felt hideous, so peeled her eyes away from the mirror.

"Two days," he replied, and she nodded. It actually did make her feel better knowing it hadn't been too long since they'd been ambushed by Tuka on that rooftop, and she turned to look at the scar from the entry wound on her back. It wasn't as long, but ran right alongside her spine, and it was a wonder she hadn't either been killed or paralyzed from it.

Kronus grabbed a notebook from a drawer nearby, and hunted for a pen while Kyra forced her eyes back to the wound on her chest and she continued to stare at her injuries via her pale reflection. She was a mess, and needed a bath, but knew she had to finish healing first, so headed back to the bed on slow and unsteady feet. Sleep would help her heal faster, she knew, and weariness soon clawed its way inside her muscle and bone as if from nowhere, but she didn't mind. Kyra pulled on a fresh nightgown and climbed back up onto the gurney, ready for some rest.

At least it's better than having a hole in my chest, she wrote on the notepad with a smile, and Kronus laughed dryly at her poorly timed joke. *Tell me why you were so angry. Was I wrong to try and save you?*

"You weren't wrong to do what you did, Kyra. You weren't wrong to do anything your entire life. I was angry with myself because I didn't deserve to have your blood on my hands. I'll never forget watching that bullet tear through you…I wished it'd got me instead," he answered solemnly, and scratched at his thick, dark beard.

Kyra got as comfortable as she could against the fluffy pillows, and she then patted the bed for him to come and lay with her. Thankfully, Kronus didn't hesitate, and she felt instantly better for having him next to her.

You're going to have to do all the talking, she wrote on the pad, and he nodded. *Where are we?*

"My home, Kro Island. This is where I've lived and worked from since Invasion Day, and is my entire life, or what little I have of one here. I've mastered the art of shutting out the world over the years, and if I can assure you of one thing, it's that you won't be bored," he answered, and looked across into her eyes with a sad smile. He was so close, and his hand cupped her cheek before he pushed it up through her hair. "I want you to stay here with me, Kyra. You don't have to decide right away, but at least tell me you'll stay for a while?" he asked, and Kyra leaned back so she could write down her response. She struggled to write without shaking, but had to know that he wasn't leading her on, or acting purely out of guilt.

I thought I was just cattle? A reject? she jotted down with one eyebrow raised in question.

"Not to me. Never to me. You know the truth

about the serum now, and I'm sorry for what happened to you and your friends. But, there are other games in play, and when things kick off, I want you here where I know you'll be safe," he told her, and started scratching at his beard again. He was always aggressive with his actions when he was overthinking things, and Kyra laughed silently at how she'd already figured out some of his tells.

When what kicks off? she asked, and Kronus dropped his gaze from hers. Whatever it was, it had to be big even if he couldn't even look her in the eye.

"Nothing, just a figure of speech. I only want to keep you safe," he answered, and while she knew it was a lie, Kyra was too tired to question him further. As with everything when it came to this mammoth man and his race, she now knew better than to push things, and guessed she'd learned that lesson the hard way. She simply gave him a nod in answer and grabbed her pad again.

Tell me something nice, a good story? she requested as she snuggled down to rest her head on his shoulder, while also pulling his hand away from his chin to stop him from rubbing it raw.

Kyra then fell asleep listening to him tell the story of how as children, he and Thrayke had once gone swimming in a lake full of poisonous frogs, and how they'd both spent weeks recuperating from the strangely potent effects in the hospital back home on Thrakor. His story provided the perfect escapism, and she let her imagination run wild with images of the pair of them laughing as they had their innocent fun.

***

When she stirred a few hours later, the huge house was dark and silent. Kyra climbed up off the bed and was impressed with her renewed strength as she stepped toward the huge window and watched the sun that'd started to rise on the horizon. Her hands instinctively went to her wound, and she flinched at the tightness of the stitches. They felt like they were already prepared to come out, and were beginning to itch. In an attempt to soothe it, she rolled her shoulders to loosen her skin and muscle, when a loud 'crack' thundered out from deep inside her chest. Icy nausea swept over her as a wave of pain then took hold of her entire body, and she immediately started to gag. Kyra ran to the en-suite and hunched over the toilet seat, expecting bile to come out of her empty stomach, but instead she looked down to find chunks of bone, bloody flesh, and even a couple of slivers of some kind of metal in the bowl. She choked and coughed up more of the disgusting refuse, and wondered what on earth could've happened within her body that would've dislodged the vile mess her stomach had somehow still been holding on to.

"What's the matter?" Kronus asked groggily from behind her, and Kyra tried to wave him away. Her voice was still gone, and she didn't want him to see what'd just come out of her, but he wouldn't go. "I'm calling Greegis. Surely that's not right?" he asked, and was still white as a sheet when Kyra had finally cleaned herself up and flushed away the evidence of her body's odd way of healing. She shook her head profusely, and mouthed her plea while trembling with fear. No matter what was happening to her, she didn't want that awful man anywhere near her ever again.

Kyra brushed her teeth and took a few deep breaths. She quickly realized just how shallow her breathing had been before she'd puked up the blood and bone, and knew something had cleared—for the better. Despite the gore of it, and the panic they'd both felt at the reaction, she actually felt better and took numerous deep breaths before heading back into the bedroom.

Not him. Never let that man near me again, Kyra demanded via her notebook, and she wrote in capitals so he knew how serious she was.

"Fine, but one day you're telling me why you're so terrified of him," he insisted as he backed off, and she shrugged a non-committal affirmation.

Kyra took a few more breaths, and felt the improvement more and more with each deep lungful of air. The stitches itched again, and she quickly decided enough was enough. They had to come out. Kronus hovered by the doorway, watching her with slowly retreating fear now that he could see she was better for having puked her guts up, but he still pounced on her when she grabbed a set of scissors from the cabinet on the wall and turned them towards her chest.

He understood exactly what she was planning on doing, and snatched the scissors from her hand. "I'll do it," he said, and when she nodded, he started the slow task of carefully snipping at the knots pulling her wound taught. Pain shot though her chest each time the scissors yanked at the wiry thread, but then it was replaced with the most wondrous sense of release when he'd pulled the knot clear, and Kyra knew it was the right decision to cut them away.

Kronus was leaning down so close to her chest that she could smell his hair, and she closed her eyes so she could breathe him in and try to forget the pain. She let her mind wander, but came back to reality quickly when she remembered what he'd asked of her the night before. Kronus wanted her to stay, but she couldn't understand why. A huge part of her wanted him to show the world what she meant to him. To defy his father's laws and make it known that she was of importance to him. But at the same time, she didn't fully know for sure whether she actually meant anything more to him than simply being another of his guilty pleasures. Kyra had even begun wondering if perhaps she was just another human object he could add to his cabinet of trophies from his time away from home.

Kronus had shown her only tiny snippets of his feelings each time he'd opened up, but then always seemed to regret it almost instantly, and would usually find a way to counteract the niceness in one manner or another.

He'd been kind and gentle since retrieving her from Tuka's grasp though, and she hoped things might stay that way. "There," Kronus's voice pulled her out of her thoughts, and she stared into his deep brown eyes for a moment before looking down to inspect his handiwork. The wound was angry and red, but the skin had already miraculously fused, and it looked far better than she'd thought it would. A thick line ran from the nape of her neck to the end of her breastbone, and she hoped it might still heal and be just a small scar at the end. On the one hand, she felt proud of her battle scar, and on the other, she felt like a fool. With no regard for the hard work Kronus, Thrayke, and the others had put in to save her, she'd almost thrown her life away. No wonder he'd been so angry, regardless of what he'd said the night before.

Kyra turned and leaned over the basin so Kronus could make a start on the wound on her back, but part of her wanted to run away and hide her embarrassment. Since she'd stormed back into his life, she'd brought with her nothing but chaos, and not once had she asked if he was ready to deal with the crazy she always had dragging at her heels.

She felt far from the headstrong and fearless woman she'd tried so hard to become over the years. Instead, all she'd given him had been a defiant, stubborn girl with no regard for hers or anyone else's safety. Kyra knew she had acted selfishly in her quest for knowledge, and realized she didn't deserve his kindness, or his hospitality. She was a fraud, and felt truly ashamed of herself.

She let herself cry, and was glad that Kronus seemed to think she was tearful from the pain of her wounds, rather than her shame. The tears stopped after a while, and Kyra swore to herself that she wouldn't hide her pain or emotion any longer. Whenever she tried to fight them, she'd failed tremendously, and promised herself she'd also stop being so quick-tempered and reckless. She'd right the wrongs she'd done, and would go back to The Tower without a fight the next time Kronus demanded it of her. A life of servitude would help her atone, and just making that promise to herself helped the darkness that'd crept into her thoughts dissipate a little.

When he was done, Kronus stood tall and stretched his back. Kyra watched him in the mirror, unable to take her eyes off him. He really was a behemoth, and she let herself watch his flawless body in awe. Every muscle was huge and defined, like a true soldier, but the way he moved was somehow graceful. The aristocracy of Thrakor had a lot to be proud of if he was a typical specimen, and she felt her cheeks burn when he caught her watching him. "I might get rid of the beard, what do you think?" he asked, and she shook her head wildly. She loved the rugged handsomeness of it, and instinctively put her hand out to touch it, but then pulled it away and dropped her eyes to the floor. He wasn't hers, and Kyra knew she'd have to get used to the fact that when he was ready to bring his betrothed to Earth, she was absolutely going to be left behind.

He noticed her hesitation, and sighed. She guessed neither one knew the best way to proceed with a relationship. Would they just be friends? Could they even be that? She was still unsure, but there was a definite attraction they were both fighting to control, and she had to admit, it felt good to feel that quickening of her heart and the flush of her skin again. Death had come close to claiming her just days before, and Kyra was glad she'd thwarted that icy grasp for a second time.

She stepped away, rolling her shoulders slowly and carefully in a bid to check for any impaired movement, and was pleased to discover the crack that'd ripped through her before seemed to be the one and only one. She turned on the shower, and then shooed Kronus away so she could get inside. He grinned, as though tempted by a mischievous thought, but then left her alone.

Ditching her dirty clothes, Kyra climbed beneath the powerful jets. The hot water stung her sensitive skin, but it was a bittersweet sensation she felt she needed, and she stood under the cascade for a long time. The sense of cleansing away the past few days was wonderful, and when she finally emerged, she felt like a new woman. With one huge towel wrapped around her body and another around her head, she walked back into the bedroom in search of something to wear, and jumped. She was certain she'd just blushed from head to toe when she found Thrayke and Domo sitting around the small table with their King deep in conversation.

Sorry, she mouthed, and reached for the nearest drawer in a desperate search for something to wear, but it was empty.

"Here, I brought you some clothes," Thrayke said with a gentle smile as he climbed up out of his seat, and he opened the bottom drawer for her. Inside were shirts and jeans, and she was glad he remembered what outfits she preferred, and her size. There was even underwear and fresh pajamas for her, and she grinned. "Wear the purple, it brings out the hint of green in your eyes," he added, handing her a checked shirt, and then he looked away before she could make a fuss of his comment. She guessed he must be just as awkward as she was about all of this, but sincerely hoped they could still be allowed to have their friendship once the dust had fully settled.

Kyra went back into the bathroom, where she got dressed and ran a comb through her almost shoulder-length hair. She left it down to dry, and then headed back out to the bedroom again. The three men all looked up at her and smiled as she reached them, evidently pleased to see her up and about. Rather than feel good under their gazes though, she felt like a mix between a prized pet and a child. They'd hushed their conversation for the second time, and Kyra hated being left out of the loop. Forcing the blues away, she joined them at the table and raised an eyebrow, daring any of them to stop her, and was glad when none of them said a word.

"I'd like an expert to come and check her voice. Everything else seems to be almost healed apart from that. If she's going to end up as a mute, we at least need to know so we can figure out what to do communications wise," Kronus said, and Domo nodded in agreement.

Although he was right, Kyra hated the idea that she might never speak again. She had to believe her voice would come back, and tapped the center of the table to get his attention. He frowned when she shook her head no, but when she tapped her wrist and traced a circle there, he finally understood. "You want more time?" he asked, and she nodded.

"Okay, but I'll see what equipment we can use to help for the time being," Thrayke offered and she smiled.

Cellphone, she mouthed, and he agreed. Although primitive now, the technology in one of the simple handheld devices would be enough for her to either type out and show someone what she needed, or she could use a text-to-speech program. She'd never been able to bite her tongue before, and had to admit she was sure ready to say all the things she wanted to again, regardless of how her mouth had gotten her in trouble so many times before.

By late morning, Thrayke had found a suitable handheld device for her to use, and her thumbs were already getting a workout on the keys. The robotic voice behind the cell's software made her laugh, but it was much quicker than writing everything down, and she was glad to have some assistance while her throat finished healing. The mayhem of the last few days meant everyone was on edge, but soon things seemed as if they'd calmed down, and the conversations naturally became less serious as the mood in the house lightened.

Kronus had to go and attend to some business elsewhere on the island, but thankfully Thrayke stayed behind and kept her company for a while. She and him chatted about the truths she'd learned during her time with the rebels, and he admitted to having read the notebooks she'd written in while gathering her intel together at Tuka's behest. Kyra knew she was overdue a proper debriefing, but wasn't quite ready for her interrogation, so decided to remain an open book with Thrayke and Kronus in the hopes they wouldn't need an Inquisitor's assistance further down the road. If they were satisfied that she'd given up everything she'd learned and experienced while immersed in the rebellion, then she figured she might also be allowed to head straight back to The Tower when she'd recovered. At least that's what Kyra was hoping. Staying on Kro Island permanently seemed more like a pipedream than a reality, but she was willing to see how things panned out before making her choices.

"Gathering the survivors' stories was Tuka's idea, but I have to admit I wanted to know the truths for personal reasons. Kronus has told me more, but I still can't wrap my brain around what he's not telling me. Why is this happening? Really?" she typed, and Thrayke took a deep breath.

"It's not my division, Kyra. I'm a capturer of rebels and rogue Thraks remember? But, I do know the main reason behind the treatments Greegis has created. It's because we need something from the human DNA that some of our kind are lacking," he answered, and she was glad he was still so ready to be forthcoming with her like he used to be. His trust and honesty meant a lot to her, and this time she wouldn't take it for granted or use her relationship with him to break the rules. Kyra had promised herself that those days were well and truly over, and she meant it. "We've found the code in less than one percent of the human population, and as far as I know, there's no rhyme or reason for those who test positive for it. A child might have the gene, when no other person in their family is positive, and when we've tried to isolate it, the chromosome either fails or cannot withstand the transformation."

"You need to connect the dots so you can perfect the cure?" Thrayke nodded. "Why do you need it so desperately?" she asked via the robotic voiced handheld, and he shook his head. She hit the button on her device to repeat the phrase again, and stared at him insistently, but still he refused.

"You remember how I said I'd always protect you? Well sometimes that includes protecting you from yourself, and your perceptiveness," he answered, and stood.

She reached out and grabbed his hand before he could leave, and stared up at him pleadingly.

Thrayke sat back down and cupped her cheek with his palm. "This is beyond any human authority, Kyra. The Thrakorian hierarchy doesn't want or need human intervention. I'm sorry."

I can help, she mouthed.

"I know you can, but for now you just need to focus on getting better. That code-breaking mind of yours might come in handy with this if we find a pattern you can decode, or if we find a way to run computer-based simulations you can assist with, but not yet," he implored.

Not seeming to care whether it was right or wrong to cut her off, Thrayke said nothing more. He gazed into her eyes and his serious expression stopped her from questioning him any further. He then kissed her forehead softly and pulled her close for a hug, and she was glad he still felt he could. "We were all so worried about you, none more than Kronus. I've never seen him go on a rampage like he did on that rooftop after you'd been shot. You said you thought I was badass getting you out of that house, but I had nothing on what he did to avenge you."

She knew he was trying to change the subject, and if she was honest, she didn't have the energy to argue, so had let it go anyway. Hearing Thrayke speak so highly of King Kronus was lovely though, and she was glad she hadn't affected their friendship by inadvertently getting in the middle of them.

Kyra thought back to the fray on the roof. The moments after the gun went off were a blank, and she'd had no idea Kronus had reacted so strongly to her near-death-experience. She rested her head on Thrayke's shoulder so she could listen to his hushed words rather than respond, and he seemed to sense her desire to hear more, so continued. "We're a bunch of selfish assholes. It's part of who we are, but when something or someone threatens those we care about, I can't even begin to describe how it affects us. Predators by nature, there isn't a word for how far a Thrakorian will go to avenge those they love. He cares for you in his own way, so don't let the rest of the crap get in the way and make you forget that fundamental fact."

Kyra was surprised by Thrayke's words, but nodded against his shoulder, and sighed. She hoped all of this would start to make sense soon, but guessed she'd settle for blissful ignorance and the odd bit of affection in the meantime if that was all she could get.

"I'm tired, but I don't want to sleep. Tell me a story?" she typed, and Thrayke laughed.

"You should know by now I'm no storyteller, but I can take you somewhere pretty cool if you'd like?" he offered, and she nodded.

He led the way, her hand in his, and together they walked slowly down through the hallways and stairwells of the huge mansion. Her energy quickly faded though, and before long Thrayke lifted her up into his arms. "You know I've always got you, don't worry." She knew all right, and relaxed into his huge body as he effortlessly carried her away.

When they finally reached their destination, Kyra felt strong enough to stand again, and she followed him through a huge arched doorway where she discovered an old movie theater that'd seemingly been fully restored by Kronus and his men. Just a handful of wide, comfortable looking, reclining seats were lined up along the floor beneath the huge screen, and they looked so inviting she went straight over to the one in the center and climbed in. If she could've groaned in delight she would have, and when her companion offered her a blanket and extra pillows she immediately accepted.

Thrayke grinned and took the seat to her right, and he then grabbed a remote control from a pocket on the side of his seat. The screen came to life, and a list showing them the thousands of movies on offer greeted them. Kyra had never seen anything like it, and knew these must've been cultivated especially for Kronus's personal library over the course of his reign. Many of the titles were hundreds of years old, and she knew had to have come from the disused archives of the old world. The arts were a dying industry nowadays; their overruling species having been more focused on industry and anything else that ensured the continuation of Kronus's reign, but she was pleased to see their new leader had protected at least some aspects of the movie industry, despite it no longer having a place within his new society.

"There are so many," she said via her device, and Thrayke laughed when he spotted her awestruck expression.

"I know, far too many to ever watch them all, but he wanted to keep them regardless. What do you fancy? Romance? Comedy?"

She shook her head and pouted. "Horror? Science fiction?" he tried, and an enthusiastic nod from her was all he needed. Thrayke then flicked through the screens to where hundreds of scary movies were carefully categorized. He chose one without even asking her for more input, and together they settled down to watch it. Disgusting alien centipedes invading Earth then filled the screen within minutes, and Kyra giggled silently at his ironic choice of movie.

They continued to watch for hours, and took turns choosing the next movie to watch from the vast array in the hard drives she guessed were probably stored somewhere beneath the massive screen. By the end of the fourth film, Kyra was starving, and was glad her body seemed to have forgotten all about her awful morning spent puking up the bloody remnants of her injury. One growl from her stomach was all he needed to hear, and Thrayke called through to the kitchen on his handset. "Junk food, and plenty of it please," he said to whatever servant was at the other end, and they then settled down to watch the start of another movie while they waited for the food to arrive.

Kyra felt rude taking such liberties with Kronus's home and staff, but Thrayke seemed happy going about his cheeky day off, so she didn't let her worries burden her or ruin their relaxing day together. Being with him and having fun so effortlessly was exactly what she'd missed, and Kyra was glad they'd found it again so easily.

She wondered where the King had gotten to, but also knew there was still a planet to run, and some potential backlash to deal with following their covert operation in Istanbul. She decided against questioning Thrayke on why he was babysitting her for the day as well, and just sat back and enjoyed the forced relaxation her weary body needed, while she indulged in some of the perks Kro Island had to offer her.

With the food came their wayward host, and he seemed far more relaxed than he had in days. Kronus slid into the chair beside her, and stole bites of everything Kyra reached for. She slapped his hand away with a smile, and he eventually gave in and ordered more from his maid. The woman nodded politely and then left the three of them to it, while Thrayke hit the play button to resume the movie.

"Poltergeists, good choice," Kronus said with a smile, and he leaned in closer to whisper in Kyra's ear. "I'm here if you get scared," he told her, and wrapped an arm around her shoulders. She nestled into his hold, regardless of not being scared one little bit, and relaxed against the strange yet enigmatic man who still had her utterly spellbound.

I wish you were always here, she replied through silent lips, and cursed the heart fluttering wildly in her chest for him. There was no way this wasn't going to end well, but she was a glutton for punishment, and knew she would take whatever she could get while it lasted.

CHAPTER ELEVEN

After a few more days spent doing hardly anything more than relaxing in front of the huge movie screen with the countless films at her disposal, Kyra was almost back to her old self again. She was able to walk around for longer periods of time, and ate so much food she was surprised she wasn't piling on the pounds, but her metabolism seemed to be running at an all-time high. Even her spirits were up, and she, Kronus, and his horde of hardened soldiers were all getting along better than ever. She'd even gotten to know Domo a little, and soon saw for herself how absolutely devoted the Master Protector was to his sovereign. It was wonderful to see how well his men cared for Kronus, but Kyra had to admit she regularly wished for some more feminine company. Her thoughts often went to those few women she'd known and loved like sisters over her life, and a few times she almost asked for information regarding Samia or Brona's whereabouts, but didn't want to overstep her boundaries now that she was making a conscious effort not to push her luck with her gracious host.

Kyra's voice still hadn't returned, but the cellphone now permanently glued to her hand was a godsend. That, along with a method of tapping or clicking with her tongue to answer simple questions, seemed to be working for the time being. The use of the 'once for yes, twice for no' system was all she needed half the time anyway. That, and an angry scowl whenever necessary, but for the most part, she and Kronus seemed to be getting on wonderfully. Their friendship was flourishing naturally, and Kyra couldn't deny her attraction to him was as well.

Following a full week's rest, Thrayke came back to visit and he finally gave into her insistence that she was ready to occupy her time with more than just food and movies, so he brought her some work to do. While he didn't seem impressed at her choice of pastime, he still delivered her with everything she needed to start cracking old codes and reviewing some of the cold cases from The Tower's archives.

Regardless of him having told her it wasn't human business, she then also began her own mission brainstorming the reasons why this illustrious genetic code was outsmarting the Thrakorian scientists. She had no idea about biology or the science behind it all, but she knew codes, and getting back to them felt like the right thing to do. Being behind a computer again after what felt like forever was a welcome step forward as well, and her hands were soon flying over the keys like they'd never left them.

She couldn't work as long hours as she would've before her injury, and wasn't cracking anything with ease, but she knew it was a worthwhile start. Kyra liked knowing she was at least contributing something to their cause, even if her nightmares were still plagued by the ghosts of her past that demanded answers she still couldn't give them. The many men and women she'd failed came to her night after night, calling her a traitor, when all she wanted was to make them proud. If their deaths meant something, then at least they hadn't died in vain, however her subconscious mind didn't seem convinced. It told her so via her nightmares, and Kyra would wake every morning with more and more dread buried deep in her gut. The pain of her misdemeanors was hitting her full force, and she had no other way of trying to atone other than to work harder, seeking answers and hopefully a way to ensure no more humans were sacrificed because of the Thrakorian curse.

Kyra wasn't always sure what he was up to, but Kronus seemed busier than she would've previously thought, and he was always quiet about where he'd been or what he'd been doing when he'd return. He stopped by to spend time with her as much as he seemed able to, and Kyra genuinely enjoyed having him in her life at long last. The first few days back on Kro Island had been hectic, but things had slowly settled down, and she felt as if he was finally letting her in.

Thanks to his abundance of human artifacts, there was always something to capture her attention, and he seemed to enjoy showing off his huge collection of items. His large island was like a museum of a world that seemed as if it was from a time eons before, not just decades previous.

She was finally able to have fun for the first time in what felt like forever, and was glad Kronus was letting down those walls of his at long last. They spent at least part of every day together, and she soon felt comfortable with him in the same way she had with Thrayke while they were exploring their friendship. There were still fears dwelling in her gut, but she tried her hardest to force them away and focus only on the then and there, rather than the unknown to come.

"Show me something you brought here with you, a taste of home, or piece of art?" Kyra asked Kronus via her cellphone one night over dinner, and he smiled in a coy way she'd never seen him smile before. It was a gentle, boyish look that made him look younger, and she liked it. She'd often wondered if the migrants from his home planet were nostalgic like the humans, or if they even enjoyed arts and culture in the same way, and she thought perhaps the differences in civilizations might be the reason why he was now a collector of such historic remnants from various points in humanity's history.

"There's only really one art form we truly enjoy, Kyra. We're a race of warriors and hunters, and we cultivate our skills from childhood, but there are some who don't embrace the soldierly way of life. We have complete equality between our genders, but not all women grow up wanting to join my father's ranks, and some pursue another way of life entirely," he told her, and his smile widened as he thought about home. "Here, let me show you."

Kronus stood and took her hand. He led Kyra to a small room at the end of yet another long hallway, and showed her inside. A large leather sofa took up one side of the small room, and across from it sat a row of speakers with a sound system sat atop them. An additional device was also connected to it, and the small piece of advanced technology was unlike anything Kyra had seen before. It looked like a large version of the same cellphone she used daily, but was clearly Thrakorian-made. If he'd let her, Kyra was dying to have a fiddle with it, but she forced herself to remain patient.

She took a seat and watched as Kronus fiddled with the machine, and then gasped when the most beautifully melodic voice surrounded them. The song consumed her, and it was so lovely she let it. The voice sang in another language she'd never heard before, and yet the words washed over her and she understood the sentiment without needing them to be translated. Kyra swallowed the lump that always seemed to be in her throat and then closed her eyes. She let the wondrous sounds take her away, and welcomed the escapism such a simple activity could bring her. Lost in her thoughts, she then jumped when she felt the sofa dip beside her with Kronus's weight.

When she opened her eyes again, Kyra sucked in a sharp breath. He was sitting so close she could feel his breath as it fluttered against her cheek, and their lips were barely an inch away from each other's. She refused to make a move on him, out of both respect for his wishes and because of her fear of getting her heart broken, but she silently pleaded for him to take what she was still ready to offer him even after everything they'd been through.

Kronus stayed perfectly still, but his deep brown eyes flicked up and down between her eyes and mouth. He licked his lips, opened them as if to say something, but then bit down on the bottom one to silence his words. It was clear he was betraying himself and his upbringing by desiring her rather than his betrothed bride back home, and so Kyra decided to do the right thing. Even though she hated herself for not jumping on the opportunity to potentially have the one thing she'd dreamed about her entire life, she knew if they let themselves go down this road, they'd both regret it. She cocked her head to the side and instead planted a soft kiss on his cheek, and then quickly backed away before she changed her mind and threw herself at the mercy of that heated stare.

Kyra then focused on listening to the rest of the song, while she and Kronus looked everywhere but at one another. When it was finished, he took her hand and led her back to the dining room so they could have some dessert. Not once had either of them said a word, and she didn't have the urge to either. She simply followed his lead and enjoyed every moment she could grasp with him. Even the feel of her tiny palm against Kronus's huge one sent a chill down her spine, but Kyra knew she'd take the stolen, yet perfectly innocent moments anywhere she could. It felt good to elicit some excitement from him, whether she could act on it or not.

"That was beautiful," the robotic voice chimed from her cell at her behest when they'd returned to the dining room. "I'd like to hear more."

"You may listen to it any time you like," Kronus answered, but he kept his eyes on the bowl of chocolaty gooiness sat before him rather than stare across the table at her.

"What's it called?"

"The piece doesn't have a name. It's just a song written by one of my ancestors. And it's my mother voice you heard, singing in our ancient language," he then added, and Kyra suddenly understood his coy smile. Just like any good and loving son, he missed his mom, and it was lovely to see him let down another of his walls, even for just a moment.

***

Time healed all of Kyra's wounds, except one. Her voice seemed well and truly gone, but despite her limitations, she and Kronus managed to have full conversations via her cell's monotonous voice, and had even developed their own hand signals to converse while in public. The others around them didn't seem to understand most of their made-up gestures, and she knew why. Kronus was still private, even with his closest guards, but he had his tells. So did Kyra, however no one else had spent enough time with the two of them to notice their inside jokes. The pair saw the conveyances easily in one another as they grew closer, and made them into a way of communicating without words.

Thrayke had been back at The Tower for weeks, and she had to wonder if it was because he'd had enough of watching their friendship blossom, but hoped that wasn't the case. She needed him to be part of her life just as much as she needed Kronus, and she wasn't ashamed to tell him so.

A busy work schedule had recommenced for Kronus's team of advisers as well as Thrayke's Gentry. While the increased amount of work being sent down from London was hard on her, she tried not to let the load weigh her down too much. Whenever Kyra felt as if she was buckling under the pressure, she hated owning up to it, but would scratch her chin to tell him she needed a break. It was just how Kronus acted when he was anxious, and rather than make an issue of her fatigue, he would simply call for a break from whatever meeting or work session they were in.

She was glad he was being so attentive, and that whenever she was tired, but fighting it, he seemed to be able to tell. It was obvious to her that Kronus had a habit of being a hothead, but he'd thankfully learned early on during her stay how much it riled her up if he demanded that she go and rest. She didn't take well to his orders in general, for some reason, and guessed it was because there was still some resentment buried within that made her want to defy him—even if it was over something as simple as a small order. Instead of barking commands at her, whenever he wanted to ask Kyra if she was okay, Kronus ran his thumb over the nape of his neck at the point where her already faded scar began. She would answer with her clicks or taps, and he'd quickly call an end to their working day whenever she told him yes. Sometimes though, Kyra opted instead for a rude hand gesture meant only to make him smile and ignore his own unease, and it seemed to work. Quite a few times he'd begun laughing in the middle of an important meeting when Kyra had flipped him off from across the room, and she loved how seemingly naïve he was when it came to cursing. She quickly taught him the basics, and could never stop from laughing hard whenever he finally put them to use while shouting or commanding his shocked comrades. None of them seemed to know how to handle the changes in their King, and Domo had confided in Kyra how he much preferred his leader's softer demeanor.

"You're good for him, and I suspect the feeling's mutual?" he'd wondered aloud without a care for her flushed cheeks, and Kyra hadn't been able to deny how right he was.

***

When she was feeling up to walking for longer periods of time, Kronus took Kyra on a grand tour of his island, where he showed her all of the larger and more obscure items he'd collected to go in his array of purpose-built hangers. He had huge rollercoasters and attractions that whirred to life only at his request. There was every form of transport she'd ever heard of—from a unicycle to a snowmobile—and even a fully functioning electronic casino run by computer systems rather than croupiers. He'd evidently scoured the world looking for things that'd taken his fancy and then brought them back to his home to experience them, but there was a huge part of it all that didn't add up.

"How can you enjoy all of this alone?" she asked via her handset while they rode horses on a stunningly preserved carousel, and Kronus shrugged. He seemed embarrassed to answer, but she hadn't asked the question to make him feel bad. *It's okay,* she mouthed, and he peered down at her from his towering height with a sorrowful expression.

"It's because I'm so alone that I need these things," he replied after a few quiet seconds. "I'm the youngest of many heirs, and in typical fashion, I had the last pick of planets to reign over. I got this place—a planet full of parasites and rejects. Or at least that was what I thought, until you came into my life." Kronus climbed down off his colorful steed and pulled her close. "I couldn't stand it here before, and distracted myself in every way I could find. I came to this planet because I was forced to, and endured the first twenty years by hiding myself away and letting my advisors run it as they saw fit. Now, I'm in control for real and it feels amazing. I make the decisions, rather than simply signing off on everything the Chief of Defense asks of me. I'm growing, learning, and changing. It's about time, too." Kyra was proud of him, and the lessons he'd learned. Kronus really had changed, or so it seemed, and she was glad he'd taken charge at long last.

When he then led her away from the amusement park, she didn't hesitate to follow. Where he went, she knew she'd always go. Kyra wanted to see the rest of his mighty collection, and followed him into building after building filled with art, books, historic relics, and even religious artifacts—including bibles. Kronus watched as she traced the binds of the old works with a delicate touch, as though mesmerized by the sight. "Your religion still baffles me. How could you believe in a power so omnipotent, yet you'd never seen it?" he eventually asked.

She hoped he was asking it rhetorically, as she didn't have the energy to type out such a long response. Kyra simply put one hand over her eyes, and the other over her heart. "Seeing isn't always believing," he murmured, and she nodded. "You humans are weird." Kronus jogged away before she could slap him, and he beckoned her over to another door, but then hesitated before opening it. "This is new, but please trust I had good intentions when I put it together."

Kyra pushed him aside with a frown, wondering what on earth she might be about to see, and her heart lurched when she found a small room laid out neatly inside with a gurney and an array of medical equipment. On the table in the center was a small machine that she recognized instantly as an ultrasound. Next to it sat a screen, and she looked back at Kronus with a fearful stare. "I need to know if I'll ever hear you speak again. Please let me take a look? I even got trained up on it so I wouldn't have to call in anyone else." She knew he meant Greegis, and was actually grateful for that part, but was still annoyed that he hadn't told her.

"I'm not ready," she typed.

"For what?" he asked, and seemed surprised that she didn't want to know how the healing was going, but in all honesty the idea of being officially labeled as mute terrified her.

"I'm not ready to find out if I'm going to spend the rest of my life in silence. I'm not ready to know yet, please," the robot voice asked of him, and she rubbed her chin to silently tell him just how anxious she was. Kronus looked utterly disheartened, but didn't pry. He simply shut off the light and led her away.

"Then it'll wait until you are ready," he promised, and she knew he meant it. Despite her previous doubts, Kyra had learned to trust in his word, and instantly felt relieved that he'd listened to her plea.

***

Kyra checked through the new batch of files Thrayke had brought her again. She separated them into groups and rearranged them on the desk, pinned certain ones on a huge pegboard, and then listed the fundamentals again in her notebook, but still the answer was evading her. At times she felt close, but never quite close enough.

Her mouth moved over words unspoken, like she would once have done when mumbling to herself about a code or puzzle she was trying to crack.

There, this lady had the serum but it failed, regardless of her having the supposedly correct DNA code. This child was the same... she mused, and began making groups afresh. She then noticed an abnormality in one patient, and then another, and another. Before long, she was rifling through them all, weeding out the test successes and failures not based on the computerized readings at the end of their treatment, but on the tests at the beginning. Their initial, pre-serum DNA samples seemed to hold the answer, rather than the other way around, she was suddenly sure of it.

Next, Kyra cross-referenced the charts and re-read each patient's history, and the answer came like a lightening bolt to her chest. She'd got it. She'd figured it out.

Instead of considering what they had or didn't have, it was more a case of what they were *going* to have. Early-onset malformations weren't registered on the selected few test results, but they'd already begun. Those successfully tested for the correct sequence had less than a one percent difference in their genetic code to the others, and inexplicably it was all because of a disease that'd been the plague of the human race for the past millennia. *Pre-cancerous tissue. That's it! They weren't present in the early stages, but their cells were regenerating incorrectly already, and the serum targeted them to a point where were not only cured of the impending malignancy, but in a way that also created an artificial purity in the blood. They were then classed as failures and terminated along with all the others, when in fact, given the right alterations, their abnormalities might just be what the Thrakorian's need?*

Kyra looked up and out the window, deep in thought. Could it really be possible that after centuries spent combatting it, the disease that'd almost been cured could be the answer the Thrakorian's were looking for? She looked again, calculated it over, and was surer than she'd ever been before about her findings. Her hand went to her mouth in shock.

"I know that look," Thrayke's voice pulled her from her intense reverie, and she jumped. She hadn't even realized he was there, and her heart fluttered wildly in panic as she took in his intense expression. "Have you found something?" he asked, stepping closer.

Kyra didn't want to give the information up until she was absolutely sure of her discovery, and for some reason she actually felt too fearful to tell anyone at all. If she gave them the answer, there might be no reason to keep the test humans alive any more. In fact their need of humans might potentially cease completely. They could be gathered and separated into different groups ready for testing as soon as the end of the following day, and she had a feeling that those who tested negative for the pre-cancerous cells in their immune system would be classed as useless, and then massacred. There would be no need to bother with the pretense of society and the sectors like before, and most certainly no point in allowing the ruse of King Kronus, Earth's savior, to continue.

Kyra smiled across at her friend and, regardless of her trust in him, shook her head. She felt sick with worry, and anxious as hell, but forced herself to remain calm while Thrayke was still watching over her. She'd never lied to him about anything, and wanted to cry knowing she was keeping such a life-changing discovery to herself for even a moment longer than necessary, but her entire species' existence hung in the balance, and she knew she couldn't rush her revelation. She had to be certain before she left the fate of her kind in the hands of their alien overlords. It was obvious he knew she was hiding something, but in true Thrayke style, he seemed to make the decision to leave her be, and she respected him immensely for stopping to give her the opportunity to come clean in her own time.

She hadn't seen her old friend in weeks, and was glad to see him again, regardless of his terrible timing. He stayed and chatted for a few minutes about the inanity of his current workload, and she listened politely but gave no real input. In all honesty, she wanted him to come and sit beside her, hold her in his arms, and bring with his touch the comfort she craved. She wanted to come clean, but her experiences with the rebels came flooding to the forefront of her mind. It didn't matter that they were friends, Thrayke and the others of his kind were technically the enemy, and Kyra knew she couldn't burden him with the information she'd found and expect him to keep it quiet.

When he'd said his goodbyes and headed off to find his King, she was actually relieved. Kyra then paced the small study she was working from, and everything inside of her went crazy with the turmoil of knowing something big, and being too scared to share it.

The dead haunted her dreams again that night and each one after. The two rebels, her parents, and then Colonel Summers from Greegis's morbid facility came through from the other side to call her a traitor, a failure, and a miserable alien-lover. She tried to call out to them, to beg their forgiveness and tell them they were wrong. She hadn't lost herself in service to Kronus. If anything, she felt like she'd finally discovered the person she'd always wanted to be because of him. The secret crush she'd once held so dear was now a genuine mutual affection, she had no doubt about it any more, and wanted to protect it by keeping her secrets safely hidden away.

Her loyalty was to Kronus and his reign, but also to the furthering of both the human and Thrakorian societies she'd been taught to serve ever since Invasion Day. She still believed in that world, and didn't want it to be over. A new world led under an autonomous reign was a wonderful idea, if you were a rebel, and she knew with all her heart that she wasn't. She didn't want to be free of their rule, in fact being left without guidance and laws scared her more than giving in to death's lingering grasp. In her dream, Kyra cried out to her otherworldly tormentors for respite from their torturous visits, but they didn't listen.

"Wake up, Kyra, wake up!" she was forced awake by Kronus and his fretful voice, and she peered up at him in surprise as she blinked away the sleep. She was covered from head to toe with sweat, and tasted the saltiness of tears on her lips. Kyra knew she must've been thrashing around and crying in her sleep, and she felt more exhausted than when she'd fallen asleep beside him as Kronus had read to her.

A huge part of her wanted to curl into his arms, but the weight of her treachery was weighing too heavily on her mind. Rather than go to him for comfort, Kyra rolled out of bed in an attempt to get away from Kronus and his questioning gaze. "Are you okay?" he asked, and when she shook her head he climbed straight out of bed and gathered her up in his arms.

She was too weak to fight, and couldn't stop crying, so Kronus carried her into the bathroom, where he sat her on the closed lid and wiped away her tears. "Tell me what it is. You haven't been right for days," he pleaded, and his sincerity only made them return.

Kyra knew it was inevitable. She'd have to come clean about her findings. Whatever the resulting changes those truths would undoubtedly bring about, the time had come, but she needed something from him first. She had to know for sure—and before she ruined everything—how he truly felt. Hearing him say it just once was all she told herself she needed, and with every ounce of courage she could muster, Kyra stopped her crying and peered across at the god-like man sitting on the floor before her.

She pointed to her chest, made a heart shape with her hands, and then pointed to him. *I love you,* she mouthed, and his eyes widened, but he didn't seem annoyed or upset with her for finally saying it.

"I love you, too," he replied, and he stared back at her incredulously. Kronus seemed surprised with his admission, and Kyra smiled when she caught the redness flush against his cheeks. She wondered if he'd ever told anyone that before, and guessed not, seeing as he'd been promised to another for presumable his entire life. "No matter how hard I try and deny it, or tell myself we can just be friends—I can't do it any more."

He paced, wringing his hands, and her stomach lurched when a regretful expression swept across his features. Kyra knew before he spoke that regardless of their admissions of love, Kronus was about to break her heart all over again. "I can't offer you a place at my side, Kyra, but I will give you everything I can while we're here. It's not fair to string you along with promises of more. There's a time limit on our lives together here, but I'll do everything I can to make it the best while it lasts."

His future wife was on her way, surely that had to be it? Or else was he too ashamed to admit to others of his kind that he had fallen for a human? Doubts aplenty filled her head, and Kyra reached up, covering his hand with her own.

Why? she mouthed, and he sighed.

"I haven't told you everything, and I'm sorry. It

was wrong of me to mislead you, and I can't even begin to explain my reasons why, but...we aren't staying here—we never were. This planet was never going to be my permanent home, and when the order comes to withdraw, we'll leave Earth and never return. Your kind is not welcome on Thrakor either, so when the time comes, you'll never see me again."

Kyra saw red. She slapped Kronus across the cheek and pushed him away. In his shock, he landed on his ass and stared at her incredulously. She couldn't believe he'd dared lead her on like he had, and her mouth moved over numerous unheard profanities and insults about his selfish, immature and immoral behavior. She silently accused him of being a coward and a liar, and even went as far to say he was no King if he couldn't even be bothered to help save a world that was supposed to belong to him.

Kronus read her lips as best he could, and had clearly made out some of her pained words. For some reason, he didn't seem angry with her for them, just sad. He simply sat back against the cold tile and watched, letting her release her fury in absolute silence. When Kyra finally stopped, she reached for her cell and typed out the words she knew she might regret for the rest of her life, but that she had no other choice. She couldn't stay and play the beloved pet of a coward who'd never love her in the way she deserved. Kyra knew she'd been kidding herself to even believe their future could be anything other than the obvious, and she felt miserable at the realization that she was going to get her heart broken regardless of whether they stayed together or not.

"Better not to miss something I never had. I want to go home," she told him before storming out to gather her things.

CHAPTER TWELVE

Kronus was a shell of the self-righteous Thrak he used to be. Once upon a time ago, he'd thought he knew it all, and had even grown bored with his planet and the selfish inhabitants of it. He had come to loathe the humans so much that he'd had as little to do with them as possible, and left his armies to govern for him while he'd hid away in self-imposed isolation in wait of his father's orders to vacate. He'd thought he was happier that way too, until a blast from the past had ruined it, and him, forever. The girl with that damn scar on her cheek.

Now, he was utterly confused by the world around him, and the life waiting for him back home on Thrakor. His father had told him when he'd sent him away that Earth was nothing more than his trial run at reigning over a planet of his own. It was always going to be temporary—a research mission to discover the secrets of their race via their primitive 'cousins,' the humans. Once they had what they needed, they were ordered to leave again, and he hadn't bothered to ask for more information at the time. He honestly hadn't cared. A good soldier and ambitious heir, Kronus did as his father commanded in all things, so hadn't stopped to question the order that his youngest son was to oversee the seemingly simple, tedious mission to Earth. In fact, it'd been an honor to accept so he could prove himself to his father, but now none of it felt so black and white.

His men had hinted at their eagerness to get their

answers and leave, and it hadn't concerned them at all to think that the end of their mission might finally be nearing. Kronus had felt the same way, and had only bothered asking questions to try and figure out how long their mission might take so he could plan his return home. He was sure his Chief of Defense was more in charge of his planet than he was, but had never cared, until recently. There had been nothing worth protecting or fretting over, and yet he suddenly felt like his heart was breaking. He'd hurt Kyra and lied to her, rather than admit that she was the sole reason he'd turned it all around at the last hurdle. He'd pushed her away at every opportunity, but still never believed she'd ever have the guts or desire to walk away. He knew then how he'd underestimated her for the final time.

Kronus confided his hurt in no one, simply because he was meant to maintain the cover of the powerful leader—the cold, distant, privileged, and arrogant rich kid. But, none of that meant a thing now that the human girl he pretended to care nothing about was leaving. He cared so much it made him sick, and yet he couldn't let himself beg her to stay.

He'd watched over Kyra every day since retrieving her from the clutches of the rebels, and she'd been a breath of fresh air to his once so strict and stuffy existence. He'd known he might never have come back from the brink of war with the rebel scum if she'd died on that rooftop, and for the first time he'd truly wanted to hunt down and wipe out all of the insurgents for having almost taken her life. Before she'd taken that bullet for him, Kronus hadn't bothered to put any time or effort into their fight with the rebels. The hunt had given his men something to do, but after Kyra had been injured, he'd been ready to massacre them all to honor her.

Having her stay with him on Kro Island had

made an empty house a home, and he didn't know if he'd ever be able to enjoy the solace ever again. If only he'd fessed up and told her how he felt, rather than tell her he loved her, only to follow it up with a damning explanation of how little he was willing to offer her.

"She's leaving?" Thrayke demanded from behind him as he joined his King. His voice boomed loudly in Kronus's ears, and normally he would've picked him up on his informality, but he didn't care for any of the etiquette. He cared for nothing at all, or at least that was what he kept reminding himself.

"Yes," he mumbled.

"Yes? Is that all you've got to say? Fight for her. Make her see sense, dammit. What did you say to make her leave?" Thrayke's anger was pouring out of him in waves, and malicious replies were on the tip of his tongue, but Kronus forced his angry retaliations away.

"I told her the truth. Kyra knows we're leaving. She can't come with us, so I'd be a fool if I let her believe we could be something more than friends," he sighed and turned away. "She told me she loves me."

"Then you really are a fool, because she and I never loved each other, and yet still I moved mountains to protect her and make her see how special she was to me. I asked Greegis to give her that treatment so we could be together longer, and didn't think for even a second that it was all for nothing," Thrayke replied, and Kronus furrowed his brow. "I wanted her and you forced us apart, when in reality you weren't willing to take proper care of her. No wonder she walked away." His old friend had just delivered the ultimate kick in the teeth, and yet Kronus still couldn't bring him self to take back any of his foolish words or actions.

Thrayke had gone above and beyond for Kyra when it'd mattered, regardless of their love affair having only been a fleeting thing. Whereas Kronus had told her he loved her, while never once doing something selfless to show her how much he cared. Fresh pain radiated from within at the realization that Thrayke had done more for Kyra than he ever had.

In actual fact, Kronus didn't like being reminded of her past with Thrayke, and he felt a growl rumble in his chest at the sheer thought of them together. His old friend ignored his vicious stare, and instead continued on in his bid to give Kronus what for. "If she ever had said she loved me, I'd have turned rogue for her. I'd have stayed behind on this dying planet and loved her until the day she died, Kronus. I'd have done whatever it took to make sure we could be together, because that's what you do when you love someone. You don't just sit back and watch them leave, and you certainly don't let them go hating you."

Silence was his answer, and it was clear Thrayke took his reticence for blind ignorance. Kronus had never thought himself a coward, not until right that second, when he knew it was exactly what he'd become thanks to the emptiness he felt growing and growing from within.

Thrayke turned on his heel and left. His words had hurt, but they were absolutely spot-on. It wasn't so simple though; surely his old friend could see that? Thrayke was thinking and speaking the words of an everyday soldier and civilian, and a Thrak free to choose for himself where his life might take him. Kronus was royalty. He had a pre-arranged marriage waiting for him back home. Mariah was a worthy bride, an aristocrat, and a lady. She would accompany him when he conquered his next and final planetary prize where they would make a home together and start a family. He would rule as King until his dying day, on which his eldest heir would take over, and so on. His future was mapped out, and it didn't matter whether he wanted otherwise. There were no choices he could make for himself like Thrayke had just chastised him about. No listening to his heart, and certainly no defying his father.

Kronus stood like a statue, peering out the window at the launch bay where he knew the craft containing the other half of his heart was about to leave from. When it'd gone, and so had Kyra, he remained locked in his stance in an attempt to steady his rage. No one tried to talk to him again, and he knew it was for the best.

When he eventually went back to the achingly empty bedroom, he found a note waiting for him from Kyra, and there was a huge part of him that didn't want to read it. If she said she still loved him, he'd lose it, but if she said she didn't any longer—he knew he'd go mad from the agony of knowing he had ruined the only real thing he'd ever had. After staring at the folded sheet of paper for a while, Kronus eventually opened it and forced himself to read.

Dear Kronus,
I should've always known you weren't mine to love, but I guess a fool will always try and listen to their heart regardless of the glaring truth. You called me a fool when we met that second time, and I guess you were right. I was a fool to care for you so much, and I was an even bigger fool to think you could care for me in return. You still saved me in ways I don't even think you know though, and I'll never forget it.
I cannot leave without coming clean and telling you that I have solved the problem with the serum and its outcome. My irresponsible brain has cracked the code that will save your race, while betraying my own, and I cannot keep it to myself no matter how hard it is to give you the answer that will result in you leaving for

good.

Do not accredit me in any way with this discovery. I'd rather live the rest of my life as a nobody than ever be associated with whatever happens next. I feel like a traitor, and do not want any part in what I know must ensue once you know this truth. I can only hope that you'll take only what you absolutely have to from my kind, and then leave the rest of us to rebuild some sort of life in the wake of your departure. So, it is with a heavy heart that I must offer you my findings, even if it means you have no reason to stay on Earth any longer afterwards.

The answer is the disease my people have been combatting for centuries, and that yours has cured—cancer. In its benign state, pre-cancerous tissue wasn't even tested for in the subjects of the trial, but that is the answer. Each and every candidate has had a full bloodwork, which is where I discovered the link. Those people without any abnormal cells failed the tests, as did any with discoverable cancerous tissue. Only the small selection of candidates with the cells in their pre-malformation stage had a conflicting reaction to the serum, resulting in a positive outcome for the factors needed for your kind, and therefore their DNA sequence should be deemed a success.

That's what you need to test for, and where you'll find the answer to your race's desire for this DNA sequence. I don't know all the details as to why you want it, but I know you were willing to murder millions of humans to get it, and I cannot sit back and continue to let that happen now that I've discovered the truth.

Even after unburdening myself with this, I'll still have to hold the weight of this breakthrough on my shoulders, but I will if it means innocent people might stop being snatched in the night and left to rot in mass graves.

Whether you admit it or not, you didn't come here to save us, only yourselves. You're the ruler of a world full of nothing but stolen lives and broken hearts, but I'll still love you until my dying breath, because somehow I'm the one and only life you ever did save. That always has and always will mean the world to me.

I'll never forget the way you've made me feel, or the friendship we've known, but I implore you to please leave me alone. I need to be free of you, otherwise I know won't survive the day you leave forever.

Goodbye,
Kyra.

It was finally clear just why she'd been so distant the last few days. She hadn't known how to tell him what she'd discovered, and Kronus couldn't blame her. Her fears were right, though. Now they had the answers they'd searched so long for, they would take what they needed and go, and Kronus knew he had to send word to his father. The Thrakorian's and their rule over the Earth might've screwed her race over at every turn, but it was worth it, because this research would save billions of lives back home.

He thought about the Earth, its indigenous race, their future, and their lives. They were nothing in comparison to his people, but especially not his father, who the serum was truly for. His life meant everything to his people, and yet he was the sickest of all his kind suffering with their strange new illness back home. Even the best doctors hadn't found a way to save those affected by the strange and deadly autoimmune Ehrad disease, and this mission was just one of their last-ditch attempts at discovering what even the most intelligent Thrakorian minds could not. Despite the uncertainties, it appeared they'd finally done it, and he looked forward to seeing the pride on his father's face when he delivered him the cure he was sure had to be on the horizon.

"Domo, get me the Chief," he called out into the darkness, and his guard came in from the hallway to answer him.

"Yes, sire." He turned to go, but then hesitated. He'd evidently expected for him to change his mind, and seemed unable to stop himself from giving Kronus a nudge. "Would you like to know where she's going?" Domo offered, and his leader shook his head, scratching so hard at his beard that it hurt.

"No," was all he could bear to answer.

He then went into the bathroom, where he grabbed his shaving gear and started scraping off the thick bristles from his face in an attempt to force away every lingering remnant of Kyra and her presence. It didn't work. Staring at his freshly shaven face in the mirror only reminded him of how much he'd lost, and how the man looking back at him was nothing but an empty shell. Kronus forced himself to get showered and dressed, and then went to meet with his Chief of Defense. He wanted off this rock as soon as possible, and knew Rasmos was the best man to make it happen sooner rather than later.

***

Kyra kept her head down the entire journey west in an attempt to hide away from the gazes of those Thrakorian men and women she'd become so strangely comfortable around the past few months, many of which she'd even gotten to know a little during her stay on Kro Island. Thrayke escorted her in silence, and when they arrived in Los Angeles, he walked with her to the Crowned King Hotel. He'd given her the choice of returning to The Tower to carry on as before or taking some time out to be by herself and clear her head. She'd chosen the latter. In actual fact, there was part of her that never wanted to go back to her old life. Something angry welled within, and she knew that deep down, she didn't want anything to do with any of the Thrakorian's ever again, much less dedicate the time she had left to serving them. The hotel was the only place she could think to go where she could be alone, and Kyra was glad Thrayke had agreed to let her have some time off rather than insist she head back with him. She somehow knew she couldn't cope with even the slightest bit of stress, even if the distraction of work was appealing. He escorted her inside, and spoke with the young woman behind the counter on Kyra's behalf.

"General Millan is to stay here indefinitely. Her entire stay is at no cost to her, including any extra charges for food, amenities etc. is that understood?" he asked, and the girl nodded profusely, clearly feeling uncomfortable in his presence. Thrayke then took Kyra's hand and lifted it into the microchip scanner, and she let him move her body without so much as a questioning gaze. She felt dead inside, and stood motionless, too lost in her own thoughts to care all that much about what was going on around her. Niceties and all thoughts of playing the game had left her, but so too had her strength and determination to succeed and survive.

She wanted the ground to open up and swallow her. Somehow, she felt both numb and on fire at the same time. She was wracked with guilt, yet was trying her hardest to force all emotion away, and it was exhausting simply being in her own skin. Thrayke explained to the receptionist that Kyra was mute, and then he escorted her to her room, made sure she had her cell and a laptop ready for use, and turned to go.

Kyra knew she ought to be angry with him, if only she could find a way to care. Tears betrayed her icy façade by falling though, and her sniffles had him muttering beneath his breath about how she was going to be the death of him. He was about to cross the door's threshold when he came to a sharp stop. Instead of leaving, Thrayke shut the door, came back over and then pulled her into a tight hug. She wrapped herself in him, pressing every inch of her body against his, and she wished she could stay there forever. Kyra wanted desperately to go back to the days when they were living and working at The Tower together. Back then, they were happy and as carefree as they could be with their secret relationship. It was preferable to this chaos, and she found she'd truly missed him.

Once her tears had stopped and it was time for him to go, Thrayke peered down into her face and smiled with genuine affection in his gaze. "Take care of yourself, Kyra. I'm going to miss you," he said, and then kissed her lips as deeply as he had during their time spent in his bed overlooking London almost a year before. His passion and tenderness helped to fill some of the voids where her cracks had formed, and while the kiss was a shock at first, she let herself enjoy the familiar warmth of his lips against hers. Kyra kissed him back, and knew it was wrong to want him, but she craved at least one last kiss with the man who had given her so much.

When he pulled himself away, it was clearly by sheer force of will, and Kyra had to smile. She knew it might be the last smile she'd wear for a while, but let herself have just one more.

***

Kyra stayed in her room for days, living on room service while watching the world go by from her window. The depression she'd felt while staying in the same hotel the last time her world had fallen apart was nothing in comparison to what she felt now, and the despairing blackness that had a hold on her was impossible to shake. She ordered hard liquor to the room, rather than bothering with a trip to the bar, and then drank herself into a stupor each night. Every morning, she woke with a clear head, and cursed the serum and its affects on her metabolism and immunity to illness. She wanted to be sick, suffering with a hangover and a headache from hell, but no. The punishment for abusing her body was nothing more than a bright morning every time, and she hated it.

One such morning, Kyra got showered and dressed for the first time in over a week. She was ready to get out of the room at last, and headed down to the lobby in search of some inspiration. A team of policemen was at the desk talking with the receptionist, and for some strange reason, she panicked at seeing them there. Part of her wondered if they were about to demand she return to work or come and assist them on a mission. Nothing could make her want to go back into the fray, and she turned and walked back into the hallway, figuring she wasn't ready to face the world after all.

Kyra was about to head back up in the elevator when she spotted a face she knew all to well across the lobby to her right. Blue, the bartender who'd kept her sane and watered during her last stay was still working behind the hotel bar just like he had before. When their eyes met, his face lit up, but his expression soon turned to that of concern when he took a proper look at her. He beckoned Kyra over, but she shook her head. For some reason, she couldn't bring herself to endure his questioning either, and she ran.

"Wait, Kyra!" he called after her, and she wordlessly cursed the slow elevator for not getting to her before he did. She hit the button again and again, and even began contemplating taking the stairs to get away from him. "What's the matter? Why are you here?" he started throwing questions when he reached her, but she just shook her head.

Kyra lifted her hand to her throat and moved it in a swiping motion to indicate she couldn't talk, and Blue immediately stopped his barrage of questions. She pointed to the scarred line on her chest, and he gasped. "What happened to you? Are you mute?" he asked in surprise, and she nodded. Without meeting his inquisitive gaze, she simply patted him on the shoulder before stepping into the elevator that'd finally made its appearance, and she then headed back up to her room. Kyra guessed she'd had enough excitement for one day, and she climbed back under her sheets—where she hid until the following morning when an insistent knock at the door forced her out of bed. She flung open the door in a huff, and scowled at the visitor standing on the other side.

"General Millan, remember me?" a young policewoman Kyra recognized from the local precinct was stood staring back at her, and the woman smiled broadly in a clearly forced manner. Kyra nodded. "I know you're mute, it says so on your records," she added, and her attitude made Kyra want to punch her in the throat, but all in all she couldn't be bothered with the hassle a fight would undoubtedly cause her.

Yes, she might hate being labeled mute, but what did it matter now that her life was empty and she had nothing to hold onto, not even the job she'd once loved? "We're conducting a DNA profile, as per the worldwide agenda you may have seen on the news?" the woman carried on, and while she hadn't even watched a single broadcast, Kyra had a pretty good idea of what she might be talking about, and nodded again. "We have yours on record already, but I am required to check your room to ensure you're alone here. Would you mind?" she stepped forward regardless of whether Kyra minded or not and took a quick look around the small hotel room. Once she was satisfied, the woman left without another word, and Kyra was left wondering just what spin they'd put on the necessity of a worldwide DNA profile, so couldn't resist checking out the news broadcasts.

"To ensure you and your family are counted and rewarded during the upcoming census, we require that everyone provides a DNA sample so we can keep a record of your whereabouts. Each and every human participant will be rewarded with a year's worth of credits," the Chief of Defense was saying into a camera on a pre-recorded loop, and Kyra laughed silently while shaking her head. People were idiots if they believed that, but then so was she to have believed all their previous lies, so she couldn't judge her fellow humans too harshly.

She was about to switch off the television when King Kronus appeared on the screen. He looked tired and sad, but freshly shaven and with every one of his walls built so high she was surprised he'd ventured out of his seclusion at all. He was a shell, cold and empty, just like her. Fresh tears stung her eyes at seeing him again, but she couldn't drag them away from his ashen face.

"Thank you all for your continued loyalty and service. Be sure to come forward for the census when called upon. Also, if you have any information regarding the whereabouts of any rebels, please take the opportunity to speak with the policeman or woman who comes to visit with you. Your cooperation is key to the survival of your race, and you will be well rewarded," he said, and then stepped down from the podium and disappeared out of sight. She spotted Domo and Thrayke following close behind, and smiled to herself uncontrollably. How could she miss them all so much? They weren't her people, nor had any of them come to check whether she was okay since having left them. She'd been tossed aside and forgotten, just like those bodies rotting in their mass graves in the arid lands to the south, and yet she still couldn't bring herself to hate them.

Even though those dreadful thoughts plagued her, Kyra wasn't angry with Kronus, or the others. After all, he was doing as she'd asked and had left her alone, but she wanted so badly for him to have chased after her regardless. If only he'd promised to defy his father so they could be together, they could've hidden away to ignite the flame that they'd both tried hard to diminish. Kyra knew it was a pointless dream, but it was one she still had trouble letting go of, and part of her wondered if she ever would.

That evening, she went back down into the lobby, and this time she headed straight for the bar. Blue gave her a wide smile, followed closely by a hug, and then he looked her over.

"You look good, but awful at the same time. How is that possible?" he asked, and Kyra shrugged. He waited a few seconds, and then added, "you're really mute then, huh?" She swiped her wrist over the microchip reader on the bar, and he saw for himself what her records said. Blue didn't make a fuss, he simply poured her a beer and put it on the bar with a smile. He then showed her the sign language symbol for thank you, and grinned infectiously. "I can teach you if you'd like? Not everyone will know it, but some will."

Kyra nodded enthusiastically. She actually wished she'd stuck around the day before, but knew it was a 'one step at a time,' deal, so chose to enjoy his company rather than beat herself up over yet another mistake she'd made.

Blue evidently sensed her need for a distraction, and so started with some basics of sign language. He used a simple point and show method, but it worked, and by the end of his shift he'd taught her a decent amount of essential word signs. Kyra loved being around her fun and carefree friend again, and she watched him a smile as he tended the bar and saw to the handful of other patrons. They then chatted long into the night using sign language and her trusty cell.

Once he was off the clock, Blue joined her for a drink, but she insisted on having something stronger than beer. He seemed surprised when she asked for a shot of neat vodka instead, but rather than question her motives, he chose to join her, and lined the bar with his own parade of whiskey shots.

Progress was slow, but by the end of the night they'd caught each other up on what'd been going on with them over the past few years. She told him as much as she could without giving away too much about her relationships with two of the most infamous Thrakorian men on the planet, and Kyra felt lighter than she had in weeks following her evening with the enigmatic barman. She said goodbye not long before dawn, and climbed into bed with a much clearer head despite the alcohol. It'd been a fun night, and she guessed the first of many steps on her road to recovery.

She dreamed of blissful nothingness, which was a welcome relief after all of her fretful nightmares of late, and Kyra knew she had Blue to thank for bringing her back up from her shame spiral.

CHAPTER THIRTEEN

Every evening afterwards, Kyra could be found propping up the bar with Blue and a glass of her favorite brand of Russian vodka for company. She saw the worry in his stare at how much she could put away, but like any good barman, he ignored her sadness and kept the drinks coming without questioning her reasons why. Rather than delve into the deep and meaningful, they worked on her use of sign language every night, and within a couple of weeks she was a pro. Blue would often insist they held their conversations entirely in sign, and eventually she asked him why it was he knew it.

My little sister's deaf. We all learned so we could talk with her.

Poor thing, she signed in reply. *I bet you're a good big brother? Did you protect her growing up?*

"Hell yeah!" he cried, and they both laughed at his outburst, but then he returned to his signing. *She's the clever one, too. She's just gone off to the army to become a nurse.*

That's great, she replied, and then took her next shot. When she looked back, Blue was watching her inquisitively.

"Speaking of. Why aren't you at work, Kyra? What happened to your voice?"

Far too much to ever tell you, and I don't want to, she replied, and scratched her chin. She realized she still did it when she was anxious, and hated how she'd taken on some of the mannerisms she'd once held so dear, and that they reminded her of the one guy she really didn't want to be thinking about. *My world has turned to crap, and there's nothing I can do to salvage it. Right now, all I'm trying to do is get through each day at a time, and when the world ends, I just hope it takes me with it.*

"Whoa, that's deep," he groaned, and his brow furrowed in sad surprise. She hadn't meant to be so honest, and regretted it instantly, but knew there was no taking it back so she didn't bother apologizing or trying to explain herself. "Oh, hey. I forgot to tell you," Blue then thankfully changed the subject, and the mood lightened in an instant. "I've been asked to go to see the big boss tomorrow. Apparently I've been performing well and am up for a promotion at long last," he added with a satisfied smile, and while her first instinct was to be happy for him, she then went straight into panic mode. Kyra's instincts instantly told her this wasn't what he thought it was, and she stiffened.

Did you do a DNA sample a few weeks back? she signed, and he nodded. *And now they've just told you to come in and get your promotion out of the blue?*

"Yeah, why?" he asked, but Kyra was too panicked to answer him. She jumped up out of her seat and ran to the counter, where she nabbed the handheld device used to scan the microchips of the bar customers. She waved it across Blue's arm and pulled up his information on the small screen, desperately searching for something she could use to look deeper into his file. She then hacked one of the firewalls and tried her hardest to get further into the network, but it was no use. The bar's system simply didn't hold the information she was after. Kyra knew she needed her laptop, and contemplated running up to her room to get it. "What are you doing?" Blue demanded, and he grabbed her by the wrist to pull her out from behind the bar.

Listen to me, you can't go. Please tell me you won't go? she mouthed, and he frowned.

"Why not? Can't I have something good happen to me for a change? Don't I deserve a chance to further my own career after years and years of serving selfish know-it-alls like you and the other soldiers?" She knew he was confused by her behavior, but his cruel reply was uncalled for, and she cursed him as she yanked her arm away from his grasp.

You don't understand. Things aren't what they appear! she signed, but he didn't seem interested in her vague reasoning's.

Kyra's cell suddenly came to life. It vibrated and chirped loudly on the table before she could even begin to find a way to answer Blue's justifiable questions, and she peered down at it in shock. It hadn't rung once since she'd been given it, but she knew who had to be on the other end. She pressed the answer button and held it to her ear.

"Don't do anything foolish, Kyra," Thrayke's voice came down the line, and a shiver cascaded down her spine at the sound. It felt good to hear his gravely tone, and she closed her eyes as it washed over her. "If you get in the way of this operation, you'll be taken straight down to the nearest precinct and locked up until we're done collecting our specimens. I know you care about him, but you need to let this go." *Collecting specimens,* he'd called it. Kyra knew she was right about why people like Blue were being offered their so-called 'promotions.' They were being gathered up like the special variety of desirable cattle they were, and Thrayke wanted her to simply stand idly by and let it happen? Despite being glad to hear his voice, she hated his authoritative tone and damning words, and hung up on him.

Blue was clearly about to ask her for details they

both knew she couldn't, and wouldn't, give him, when the cellphone rang again. She pressed her finger against the answer button so hard Kyra was surprised she didn't break it, and she begrudgingly held the cell to her ear again. "Please. I made you a vow that I would keep you safe, and I'm keeping it now by warning you against acting out. Listen to me," Thrayke implored her, and she hung her head, but tapped once on the speaker to tell him yes. "I can see you. I've always watched over you, kept you safe. Don't you understand how much I care? I learned sign language right along with you, and I can read your lips. Sometimes I think you forget just how far I'm willing to go for you."

Emotions welled inside and the elation at knowing he hadn't abandoned her mixed with Kyra's anger, but it was a concoction she found hard to deal with. She still adored Thrayke, and missed him as both a friend and lover. But, at the same time she hated his entire race for going ahead with their covert plan to syphon away their choice of strategically DNA profiled humans for their personal use. "Go to bed, Kyra. Say goodbye to your friend and walk away."

Please make sure he isn't harmed, or that it's at least quick and painless? she mouthed, and knew he was watching via some hidden camera somewhere when Thrayke agreed to do what he could.

Kyra hung up the phone and handed the chip reader back across the bar to the waitress on duty. She then ordered herself a bottle of vodka to go, and sat back down at the booth opposite her friend. *I'm sorry for how I reacted. You're an amazing guy, Blue, and you deserve to go far. You'll go down in history yet, I just know it,* she told him with a forced smile, and kissed his cheek. She then hugged him tight and went upstairs to her room before he could see the tears that were more than ready to fall down her cheeks.

In her room, Kyra switched on the TV news channel. She turned off the sound, and just watched as the images flashed across the screen. They were the powerful men whose faces she knew so well it hurt, and yet she couldn't bring herself to look away. She sat on the end of her bed for hours, staring at the footage as it played on repeat while swigging from her bottle of vodka. She wished she could drink enough to numb the pain, but knew there'd never be enough liquor in the entire world to successfully do that.

When the early morning sunrise appeared out her window, she stared into the bright sky for so long her eyes grew sore. With one last sup, her bottle was dry, and she got her wish at last. A new day had begun and she was sick. Her head was pounding and her stomach wanted to heave up its heavy slosh of booze, but she welcomed every second of the wretchedness. Kyra felt she deserved the sweet agony of the hangover she'd evaded for weeks. She wanted every awful moment of it, and actually wished she could find some more alcohol to ply her body with so that she might successfully take herself over the edge and into complete and utter queasiness. Her ghosts hadn't come to taunt her, thanks to the lack of sleep, but the pain had. It radiated outwards from her chest, and was a pain that had nothing to do with her old wounds. She felt like it was clawing at her from the inside, ready to come out, but she didn't care. Nothing mattered anymore but the emptiness. The wonderful, freeing, numbing emptiness.

With her eyes on the sky, she failed to notice when the door of her room opened and a darkly dressed figure stepped inside. It was only when the figure was right next to her and he wrapped a hand around her throat that she gasped in shock at the presence, but even then the fight had left her. Kyra prayed to be released from this world, her torment, and her loneliness. She wished for the peaceful oblivion she'd tasted so many times in her pitiful life to return, but the relaxed grip on her neck told her that whomever had invaded her solace wasn't there to kill her. She let her head get tilted back, and she peered up into Thrayke's intense gaze without a care for what state he'd found her in.

He looked angry, but she couldn't figure out why. After all, she'd let Blue go to his death without so much as another word to try and stop him, which was exactly what he'd ordered her to do. Thrayke watched her for a few seconds, and then leaned closer, folding his tall body so that his lips found her ear.

"Stay away, I told myself. Stay far, far away from her, and yet here I am," he groaned, and his voice was almost a growl. "He left you to rot here like a discarded and unwanted pet, but I can't do it. I had to see you, to tell you that no matter how bad you're feeling, you did the right thing." He slumped down on the bed and cradled her from behind, while Kyra remained motionless before him. Part of her wondered if she'd fallen asleep and that it might be a dream. She didn't want to chase him away by moving or trying to converse with her vision like always seemed to happen in her dreams, so she remained perfectly still. His powerful words were a welcome rose among all the thorns that'd surrounded her, and she wanted to hear more. "You're not a reject. You're everything to me, and I need you to know it. Who was there for you when no one else was? Me. I protected you from Greegis, and I rescued you from Tuka. I brought you here to save you from yourself, but I can't save you from me, Kyra. Do you understand?"

She nodded, and his grip around her neck tightened as he sucked in a hiss. Thrayke pressed his nose against her temple, and kissed the scar on her cheek. "I know you love him and not me. I have to accept it, but at the same time I hate you for letting him steal your heart when he doesn't intend on keeping it. He'll go home and never look back, while I'll regret leaving you behind until my dying breath. I wish I could make you happy again before I go. I wish I could take your pain away and fix you. I wish you'd let me."

Kyra clicked her tongue once in affirmation, and Thrayke sighed deeply.

I can't, she signed, and he watched from over her shoulder. *I just...can't.*

"I wish you wanted me like I want you," Thrayke groaned, and Kyra could see from the corner of her eye that his face was knotted tightly in his angst. His pain made her feel better somehow, and she felt her passion for him begin to radiate from within again. She waited for a second, trying to think of all the reasons why she shouldn't do this, but none of them were strong enough to stop her. Thrayke was right. Kronus had thrown her away and hadn't fought for her when she'd needed him to, whereas Thrayke had always fought to keep her safe and in his life. He'd shown up out of the blue to tell her how he felt now, and her heart was telling her to go for it with every beat it gave.

She put her hand over the one still holding her neck, and he instantly loosened it. She knew he thought she didn't want him to hold her, when it was just the opposite. Rather than pull it away, Kyra then slid his palm down over her breast and waist to rest on her thigh, and then turned to stare into the powerful blue eyes of his that were mere inches away from hers. She lost herself in his oceans, but somehow found herself there, too.

I do want you, she mouthed. *I've always wanted you,* she added, and then leaned in to kiss him. Thrayke didn't second-guess her or hold back for even a split-second. He pounced on her, and had Kyra seeing stars within minutes thanks to the lack of oxygen, but she didn't care. She gave him everything he wanted, and unlike Kronus who'd pushed her away at every affectionate advance, Thrayke took all that she had to offer without question or any hesitation. He gave her the care and attention she'd craved and been denied. Together, they were as passionate as they'd once been, but also so much more. The past torment gave them each a new, darker need, and they explored it together willingly.

Thrayke worshipped her body and enjoyed her in ways his King had never known. The connection was their wonderful secret once again, and Kyra lost herself in him. What was left of her heart beat only for the merciful soldier who'd come to her in her darkest hour, and she let him consume her entirely. It was truly freeing to give herself over to him, and Thrayke helped heal her by tending to her needs in a way only a truly dedicated friend and lover could.

Only when the sun started to set again did they come down from their crazed high, and Kyra felt light and free at last. Before falling asleep, she tensed in panic, and Thrayke seemed to sense her unease without even having to ask.

"I'm not going anywhere," he told her, and she then fell straight into an exhausted sleep wrapped in his warm and safe embrace.

***

The next morning, Thrayke ordered room service while Kyra soaked in a hot bath. Her hangover was long forgotten, but a blissful and euphoric emptiness lingered that was a welcome side effect of her day spent with her mighty lover, and if she could've groaned in delight she would have. When she finally emerged, a veritable banquet greeted her, and she grinned.

"I couldn't decide what I fancied, so I just ordered one of everything," Thrayke told her with a boyish grin. He looked cheerful and relaxed, and Kyra knew her smile must've shown him the same elation, because he immediately swooped up from his seat and took her mouth for a deep kiss. When the two of them were together like this, Kyra was truly happy. If she could do it all over again she hoped she'd do things differently, and yet couldn't hate Kronus for having made her fall for him, but wished things hadn't ended the way they had. There'd been no proper goodbye, only pain, and she knew those cracks in her heart and soul might never truly heal.

She forced herself out of her melancholy, and sat down to start her taste-testing session of the variety of foodstuffs Thrayke had ordered for them. Bites of each wonderful plateful were taken without a care for etiquette, and she grinned across at him as they devoured their huge breakfast. Thrayke was the same, and armed with nothing but forks, they tucked in without a care in the world.

Now that you've started rounding up the humans with the compatible DNA sequence, does that mean you'll be leaving soon? she signed when they'd finished, and was grateful for his honesty when he replied.

"Yes, and within a couple of weeks I'd imagine," Thrayke answered, but looked away as he spoke the finite words. While she appreciated hearing the truth at long last, Kyra couldn't help but feel her mood darken a little at the realization that before long, he too would be out of her life for good. He'd been a constant presence in her world ever since the day she'd gone to The Tower and been thrown into the life of a Gentry officer, and she now knew the measures he'd gone to so he could protect and care for her the entire time between then and now.

They both shook off their misery and chatted about better things, albeit forced, and soon they were laughing and reminiscing about their first few awkward weeks together in London when their connection had begun. Thrayke also told her some more stories about his home, upbringing, and his adventures as a soldier, and Kyra wordlessly responded without a care for her lost voice. He kept up with the lip-reading wonderfully, and before they knew it, they'd whiled away the entire morning.

You'll get in trouble if you stay here too long, she eventually told him, but Thrayke shrugged it off.

"I don't care. I'll tell them I was on a private mission to collect my personal effects. No one will care anyway now that we're starting the drawdown." He pulled her close and kissed her lips. "You're more important than that damn Tower, or the people in it."

***

Thrayke went back and forth from her hotel bed and The Tower over the following week, and Kyra got used to having him come and go in his odd commute between London and Los Angeles. She was thankful he had such a high-speed hovercraft for his use, and spent the remainder of her stay feeling happier than she had in far too long. In fact, she couldn't remember ever feeling less burdened, even if she was being selfish by keeping him to herself during his final days on Earth.

She wasn't sad to say goodbye though. It no longer mattered that he was leaving, because she'd already made some important decisions that'd helped take the weight from her shoulders and the ache from her heart as well. When the ships left Earth, Kyra planned to throw herself off the roof of the hotel. She didn't feel she belonged with the humans any more than she belonged with the Thrakorian's, and knew that someone without a place to call home was more dangerous than someone fighting for the wrong cause. Kyra knew she'd do something foolish if she tried to live a proper life after they'd gone. She'd do something stupid like owning up for her crimes against her race out of guilt, and she couldn't bear to spend the rest of her life being hated or locked up because of her betrayal. She'd much rather die, and so had chosen that path. Kyra felt as though she truly deserved for her life to end, and that it was symbolic to do it when the Thrakorian's she adored left her forever. It was a way in which she could serve the King she still irrationally yearned for right until the bitter end. She was a fool, but it was evident now that she was a stubborn fool who refused to learn her lessons and move on, and that the world would be better off without her.

"Do you remember what you learned in your training about Thrakorian men?" Thrayke asked her one evening with a coy smile. She searched her mind for the answer, but he revealed it anyway. "When they fall in love, it's with one person, and it's for life. They stay loyal to their one lover and put them above all others. That's you, Kyra. You're mine," he told her, and he held her tightly to his chest as though she really were his most prized of human finds. "I fought it, believe me I did, but I eventually decided it was time to stop fighting my feelings. Even back in The Tower when we were chatting about everything and nothing, trying to be friends—I knew." He sighed deeply, and buried his face in her hair, and Kyra squirmed as his breath tickled her neck.

She wanted to look at him, to see the emotion in

his eyes, but he held her still, as though he didn't want her to see as he poured his heart out to her. "I knew it when you were lying in Kronus's bed night after night, regardless of nothing having happened between you two. I forced myself to respect your choice to stay with him, and his order for me to stay away. I know now I should've told you how I felt, instead of just acting like some kind of cold ice-man, but when it comes to him, I have no argument. He chose to keep you as his own, regardless of offering you nothing in return, and I couldn't object. But now? I want to scream it from the rooftops and tell the world you're mine, because I love you, Kyra Millan. I always have and I always will."

She didn't know whether to laugh, cry, hit him, or kiss him, but one thing was for sure, Kyra knew she felt the same way. Her affection had gone in two directions her entire life. Even back when she'd been with Silas, she'd still had her crush on the King that she'd held dear since Invasion Day. Like the others, Silas hadn't even known he was competing with another for her affection, and neither had Thrayke when they'd begun seeing one another the first time around.

The decision never to tell them her full Invasion Day story had been Kyra's choice, but it'd only served to keep Kronus on the pedestal she'd created for him. She knew now how they'd never stood a chance. Her adoration had meant all her other partners had lived in Kronus's shadow, but not any longer. The past few months had been tough as hell, but she'd gotten through them and could see the truth at last. Kronus said one thing, while meaning another, and then doing another thing entirely. He was never going to give her anything more than he already had, while she'd devoted her life to him. But no more.

Knowing that Thrayke felt that way about her was a comfort she felt selfish for needing, but instead of hiding, Kyra embraced it. She might've shied away from self-indulgence in the past, but that was when she was a foster-kid from the slums who didn't want to own up to the fact that she was suddenly thrown into the life of an upper-class human. She'd hidden away from her wealth and status because she'd felt guilty for enjoying it when so many of her fellow orphans were still poor and uncared for.

However, she refused to play the martyr any longer. Kyra endeavored to spend her last days enjoying the life she'd earned, and she decided to let go of her emotional baggage once and for all. One man had earned her love and loyalty, and he would have them both until she took her last breath.

I love you too, Thrayke. I always will, Kyra mouthed when he released her, and she then kissed him with all the passion and adoration she could muster, just so he'd know she truly meant it.

CHAPTER FOURTEEN

Thrayke docked his craft at The Tower and then headed straight for his private quarters. In his mail, he found a memo regarding the evacuation of his kind from Earth, and saw right away that his Division were due to commence their retreat the following evening. He didn't bother to read the rest though, and smiled to himself as he tossed the slip of paper back down onto the desk. None of that mattered, not any more.

After carefully sifting through his few belongings to neatly sort them, he packed a bag with only the essentials he knew he'd need for his next, and final mission. His collection of relics would go aboard the mother ship the following day, and although he would miss them, he knew there were more important matters to be addressed first. Thrayke had made up his mind. He'd decided before even going back to see Kyra that he wasn't leaving without her, and now that she'd confessed her love for him, he was absolutely sure of what he wanted to do next.

Instead of dragging her away with him, he'd decided it was time they both escaped Kronus and his reign for good. Jealously had made him act rashly in the past, but this didn't feel the same. Thrayke had a cool head at long last, and knew he'd made the right choice. He was going to stay behind on Earth with Kyra. It didn't matter that she was rebounding, or that her depression had forced her into his arms. She was coming back to him, bit by bit, and that was all that mattered.

Saving her hadn't ever been for personal reasons, but Thrayke knew he would gladly reap any benefits she afforded him in return for all his hard work. It'd been worth the heartache, and she was certainly worth giving up everything for.

He let his mind wonder about how they might live after his kind had deserted her planet. They would have to hide away, perhaps even join colonies of other rogue Thraks—wherever they might be—and wasn't that just so ironic? The powerful and resolute Besieger, capturer of rebels and rogues, would go to join the ranks of those he'd spent the past two decades fighting against. They'd become his new family, if they let him in of course, and he'd gladly choose a life spent proving himself to them over being alone and missing Kyra for six or seven hundred more years back home.

Despite his bags being packed, Thrayke knew he couldn't head out again quite so soon after returning. He grabbed his paperwork in a bid to try and keep his mind occupied until he could slip away unseen, and he started taking anything that might help them. He decided he'd start by doing whatever it took to find Kyra a safe new home, a place where she could feel welcome, and a world in which she might even want to start a family someday. It was the perfect plan, and the chaos of the Thrakorian evacuation would provide the perfect cover for his disappearance. All Thrayke had to do now was bide his time, and then without a word he would slip away into the night to go and start his new life with Kyra by his side.

He decided to pre-empt his search for any rogues, and combed his leads for any useful information regarding their whereabouts. Kyra would be able to help him crack some of their codes, and he stashed the files, ready to take them for her to look at when she was ready.

By morning, he had everything ready to go in

his pack. He decided not to tell a soul he was leaving, not even Kronus. Thrayke knew his leader and friend would try and stop him, perhaps even by force, and the last thing he wanted was to have to fight his way out of his old friend's strong grasp.

When all was ready to go, and his countdown had begun, Thrayke sat at his desk with his hands beneath his chin. He took a good look around his office, and surveyed the past two decades' work. He'd served his sovereign well for centuries, and would miss him, as both his trusty companion and as his King. Kronus was a great man, but he'd let himself become blinded by his royal status, and he'd let everything his heart had truly wanted slip away. His head had ruled him instead, and Thrayke knew that a huge part of that was the figurative sound of his father's voice in the back of his head that scolded Kronus for even daring to go against his orders. As much as he respected and revered King Thrakor, he had always been an impossible man to please, and the youngest of his heirs had let his disappointment affect him far too much over the years.

Kronus had pushed Kyra away, and they'd all seen how badly it'd affected him, but he'd not once gone back on his word. Thrayke knew he might never be the same again, and was genuinely sorry that he wasn't going to be around to help his old friend get through the tough times ahead.

Thrayke thought of Kyra again, and how he'd made sure he was always the one there to catch her when she fell. He'd watched over her day and night, and had only stepped in when he couldn't take watching her self-destruct any longer. For a mute, her body language spoke volumes to him, and he could see for himself how she was spiraling. A dark cloud had hung above her head at all times, and even from afar he could see that it was wearing her down. Kyra had stopped caring about anything, even herself, and he knew it was time he took charge. He'd do everything he could to stop her depression becoming dangerous, and a flutter in his chest reminded him of his admission the day before. She truly was his one and only, and he didn't regret those words of love he'd spoken for a second. Thrayke knew without a doubt that not only that he would die for Kyra, but that he would also die if he ever lost her.

"Women," he muttered to himself, and laughed gruffly. "Enigmas the lot of them, but my goodness it's worth it." Thrayke sighed and scanned the memo that'd been left for him again, and he checked his watch. According to the itinerary that was meticulously planned out before him, the last of the viable human specimens should be being loaded into their transporters. They'd reach the once dormant stasis-chambers aboard their main ship situated just above the Earth's atmosphere within the hour. The humans who'd tested positive for pre-cancerous cell mutation during the census were already sedated after being lured to the various treatment facilities, and they would remain on ice until they reached Thrakor. There, they would be housed in vestibules specifically designed to preserve their life expectancies, and their bodies would be tested comprehensibly so that Greegis and his team could complete the 'extraction phase' of the experiment.

Thrayke wondered how their mother ship was holding up after all the years spent in storage, but he also knew an entire team had been charged with caring for the gigantic vessel throughout their earthly stopover. Each of their Thrakorian crafts had been stored on the country once called Ireland to the west of their hub in England for the past twenty years, and should've been cleared for takeoff by now—provided they were full to capacity of the relevant teams. According to the memo, all Thrakorian's and mixed-breeds were allegedly packed up by now, and should be ready to go once the final signal came. They would then travel to the mother ship in smaller hovercrafts and dock once outside the Earth's atmosphere, where they would then begin the long journey back to Thrakor.

As he read on, he noticed a sentence at the end, and reread it with a frown.

'Lastly, Project Preserver will be withdrawn, and Earth will resume its previous countdown.'

He'd never heard of 'Project Preserver' before, and wondered why. Thrayke knew there wasn't much time to spare, but that he also needed to know everything about this illustrious undertaking if he were to be sure about staying behind. He looked it up on his computer, but there was nothing about the project or why it'd even been put in place. Frustration was creeping into his usually so stoic demeanor, and Thrayke knew it was because there wasn't long left for him to gather his final piece of intel. Because of the lack of time, he did the only thing he could think of before having to ask for clarification on it from above, and he hacked his way into the very computer system he'd helped design. He hazarded guesses at what his kind might've put into place to 'preserve' the planet, considering ongoing issues with the lack of fossil fuels or sustainable food sources, but what he found made him curse loudly at his computer.

Thrayke covered his mouth in shock when he read on, and stared dumfounded at the documents on the screen before him. *Why wasn't I told? Why is this the first time I've learned this truth?* he thought. A million other questions flew through his mind, but so too did an abundance of new fears. He wasn't sure whether he'd make it back to Kyra in time, or if he could get out of The Tower unseen earlier than he'd planned, but Thrayke knew he had to at least attempt it. He'd die trying if he had to, but the promise that he might just get back to her before it was too late made him move his old bones quicker than ever before.

***

"This is a public service announcement. A notification for a worldwide blackout has been issued for this evening, and all human civilians are hereby warned that they must stay in their homes for the duration for their safety. Essential relocation of electrical systems is being carried out, and please rest assured that the disruptions should not last long. Thank you," a softly spoken Thrakorian spokeswoman spoke directly into the television camera with a fake smile, and when the simple recording then started to replay again and again, Kyra turned off the television and peered out the window at the horizon. Dusk was just falling across the city, and Thrayke still hadn't returned. She wondered where he might be, or if he was even able to come and say goodbye in all of the chaos after all. She desperately wanted to see him again before his race disappeared, but wasn't sure there'd be time.

Kyra guessed the supposed blackout had to be a cover story so that their ships could power up and take off across the world unseen—it had to be. And it could mean only one thing. The Thrakorian's were finally leaving her planet behind, and instead of being sad, fresh anger spiked in her gut. Regardless of her still lost voice, she wanted to scream and shout profanities from the rooftop at their ships as they departed, and soon found herself climbing the stairs up to the roof on autopilot.

Out in the cool twilight air, she peered up into the heavens and took in the ancient beauty of the stars. It was unusually quiet, and a tiny breeze rustled her shirt, but otherwise the Earth seemed remarkably still. She wondered if perhaps it'd stopped turning at all, or if it wasn't just her who instinctually knew that the end was near. Kyra then watched as the sun finally set behind the skyscrapers in the distance, and then saw as lights began turning off all over the so usually bright and bustling metropolis. It was only minutes until utter blackness had descended. She then heard what sounded like the hum of a thousand bees coming from all around the city, and Kyra smiled to herself. She'd proven herself right once again. In the darkness, there was nothing she could see with the naked eye, but her ears knew the sound well, and she watched the night's sky as it blurred here and there from what was clearly an influx of hovercrafts slowly heading up into the atmosphere to join their people. It was time. They were leaving, and there wasn't anything she could do about it.

A large star seemed to be moving slowly across the sky far above her, and she watched it for a while. There was something otherworldly about the beacon, and it somehow seemed as if it was waving down at her like a thief that'd ran away with her prized belongings in plain sight. Kyra knew it couldn't be a shooting star as it was moving too slowly, so she guessed it had to be the Thrakorian mother ship.

Go! Run back to your home with the answers I gave you because your minions were too stupid to analyze every detail. You're a coward, Kronus. A bloody coward, and I'm ashamed of ever loving you... she cried silently into the darkness.

Her lungs burned as if she were actually screaming out the words, but still no sound came from her useless throat, and she cursed him for having stolen her voice along with her pride. Kyra felt ashamed of the person she'd become because of King Kronus and his army of cowards, and she hated how her sacrifices had all been underappreciated in the end.

Lives had been lost—so many innocent people murdered for their cause, and all for nothing. The humans' loyalty had meant nothing, and now they were simply being tossed back into the scrapheap because they'd served their purpose. The Thrakorian's didn't care whether the humans survived in their absence, and she tried to convince herself that she didn't care about their race in return. *You took everything from me, you asshole, and gave me nothing. I hate you! Good riddance to you all. I hope you never come back,* she mouthed, and gripped her stomach as it panged with despair. She was well aware she was spouting lies, and decided it was almost time to wash her shame away one final time.

Kyra stepped up onto the edge of the roof and looked down the hundreds of feet to the ground below. Tears streamed down her face and her heart broke all over again, but she refused to die a weak and feeble shell of the strong woman she'd once been. Memories of her lying wrapped in Kronus's embrace overwhelmed her, and she rubbed her chin absentmindedly.

Despite her angry thoughts, she already missed the man she'd once hoped to find a way to love. He'd kept her safe, and taken care of her in a way that'd made her fall for him, and it'd confused the hell out of her. Kronus had held her close and spoken of his adoration for her, and yet never been willing to put her above anyone else in his own race. She felt like such a fool to have ever believed his attentiveness might possibly be genuine, and wished she could find a way to forget him completely. Kyra wrapped her arms around herself and cried some more. Kronus was nothing more than a spoilt and arrogant little prince, and she tried one last time to convince herself that she hated him.

She thought instead of Thrayke, and let her pain turn to longing. She truly wanted him above all others, and smiled as she let herself think of his arms as they'd wrapped around her, his kiss as he showed her how much he cared, and the heart he'd declared was hers for the taking...

The lights returned almost as soon as the buzzing had finished, dazzling her. Out of nowhere, the ground then began to shake beneath her feet, and Kyra stumbled forward, closer to the building's edge. She thought she might actually fall, and quickly realized that despite her once so steadfast suicidal plans, she wasn't actually ready to die. At first, she guessed the vibrations must be something to do with the crafts all having taken flight, but then she remembered how she used to feel tremors like this regularly as a young child. What she'd felt was an earthquake, albeit a small one, but they hadn't had them in twenty years, and it was a shock to be standing atop a building that was somehow rattling uncontrollably beneath her.

An eerie silence fell, and then another tremor started, this time stronger than the last. Kyra lurched forward again, and readied herself for the fall to her death she guessed was imminent, but jumped when she felt strong hands grip her waist and pull her back from the edge.

"What are you thinking?" Thrayke bellowed at her when he'd yanked back onto the safety of the rooftop. Kyra couldn't answer him. Instead, she flung her arms around his shoulders and held on tight. He'd come back, even if it was just to say goodbye, and she felt an amazing sense of closure now that she'd had the chance to see him one last time.

It's okay. You can go. I'm so glad that I got to see your face again before it's all over though, she mouthed, and pressed her lips against his. Thrayke kissed and hugged her back so hard the breath left her lungs in a rush. It was exactly what she'd been missing, and she guessed he felt the same because he crushed her body into his as he caressed her. They were both lost in their moment, and it was only when another tremor shook the building a third time that she finally pulled back. Kyra looked up at Thrayke in shock, desperate to know what was happening, but he didn't say a word. He held her close again, but it was only when her immensely powerful lover lifted Kyra off her feet and was throwing her in the backseat of his hovercraft that she realized he'd abducted her. *No!* she tried to tell him, but he simply shook his head.

She wanted to demand that he release her, but then she peered into his deep blue eyes and paled. Thrayke was watching her with an expression she'd never seen on his face before—fear. He buckled her in tight and then climbed into the pilot's seat in front of hers, and they were airborne before she could even loosen the belt, let alone try and escape. Kyra kicked the back of his seat to get his attention, but he ignored her. With skilled piloting techniques, Thrayke took them up into the clouds a heartbeat later, climbing higher and higher at breakneck speed, but all she could see was the back of his head.

When she felt more pressure hit her chest, she knew they'd hit the first layer of Earth's atmosphere, and immediately stopped fighting his kidnap. It felt like an elephant was sitting on her, and Kyra sucked in breath after breath in a bid to stay conscious, while he seemed completely unaffected by the changes in pressure.

"Just take deep breaths, okay? We'll be there soon. I'm going around to find a different dock in the hope we don't find any others there," Thrayke called over his shoulder before he focused again on the task at hand, and Kyra felt the small craft swing to the right. "I knew all along that I couldn't bring myself to leave you there alone, Kyra. I was coming back no matter what.

But it looks like you had other plans, huh? I was going to stay behind with you. Do you realize how much I was willing to give up to be with you? And you were ready to just throw your life away," he demanded, and she could hear the anger in his tone as he ranted question after question they both knew she couldn't answer. She stomped her foot once, indicating yes. She had intended on killing herself, until the literal do or die moment. She also understood exactly what he'd done for her, and Thrayke sighed.

Kyra wasn't going to deny her true intentions on that rooftop, and he punched the roof of the cockpit in his rage. "We'll talk about this properly later, but right now I need you to do exactly as I ask. If you're discovered, we'll both be in big trouble, so for once can you do as you've been told?"

She stamped her foot once in affirmation again, and saw him nod in approval. Her head was pounding. Fear, guilt, anger, and the utter loss of all she once knew were overwhelming her, but somehow the love she felt for the man who'd saved her once again crept in, too, as well as her instinctual desire to survive. She knew how much Thrayke was sacrificing to save her, and felt indebted to him in ways she knew it'd take her a hundred years to repay, even if he never let her.

Kyra had been so sure that she'd wanted to die, but now that he'd saved her, she felt the exact opposite. Every part of her wanted to hug and kiss her alien savior in thanks, but she also wanted to slap him for being foolish enough to save her. His life could've been so much simpler without her in it, and part of her wished he hadn't burdened himself by stowing her away. She wondered how he even planned to hide her on a ship filled with Thrakorian soldiers, or whether he'd actually thought that far ahead.

Kyra guessed it might've been a knee-jerk

reaction to grab her and throw her in the craft, or had he already decided to take her along with him. She couldn't be sure, but he'd also said he was planning on staying, so Kyra found herself wondering why he hadn't flown them both somewhere secluded and safe on Earth rather than heading up to the mother ship bound for Thrakor. Her mind was running wild with questions unanswered, and they only served to make it pound harder.

Kyra shrunk back in her seat and watched through the tiny sliver of window as their craft moved through a pressurized dock and then landed in a dark hanger. Inside were hundreds of small crafts that'd already been cleared, cleaned, and stored, and thankfully the place seemed locked up and empty. "These are the ships from Australia and Asia. The owners are already tucked up in their quarters ready to watch the show." He turned back in his seat and watched her intently, as though contemplating what to do with her now that he had successfully stolen her away.

What show? she mouthed, and frowned when he couldn't meet her gaze.

"You'll see," was all Thrayke answered, and he jutted his chin towards a large black lockable box in the back of the craft. "Get in there."

Kyra did as he asked, still too dumfounded to answer him back or question his motives. It was clear he intended to carry her in masqueraded as just another part of his luggage, and she hoped he was planning on being gentle with his fragile cargo. There wasn't much room to move around in the dark case, but it was airy enough that she didn't feel claustrophobic, and so Kyra forced herself to stay calm and take deep breaths when he closed the lid.

Before long, Thrayke began pulling it along on its wheels by the handle, and within minutes Kyra could hear that they were amidst a bustling convoy of men, women, and children who'd docked along with them. She could tell without having to take a sneaky peek that people who would turn them both in without hesitation surrounded them, so she kept perfectly still despite her legs already having started to grown numb and uncomfortable.

It wouldn't matter that Kronus had a soft spot for them both, their betrayal would surely be met with severe punishments, or else he'd look weak in front of his patriots. The only person Kyra knew she could rely on was Thrayke, and vice versa. He was her everything, and regardless of how they'd gotten here, she was glad he'd decided to save her after all.

CHAPTER FIFTEEN

What have I done? Someone will figure it out, and I'll get us both killed... Thrayke's thoughts were running away with him, and he had to take a few deep breaths before he could press the button that would tell the elevator which floor he wanted to disembark on. With two bags hoisted across his back, and two huge suitcases dragging behind him, he knew he looked like nothing more than another Thrak who'd grown attached to a few things from his new life and wanted to take them with him back home. It wasn't too far from the truth regarding his most precious cargo, and he was careful not to bump her along too much on his way to his quarters on the upper-level of the ship.

He nodded to the few people he saw along the way, but didn't stop to chat. Thrayke almost made it to his doorway when a voice he simply couldn't ignore called for his attention.

"There you are. I was beginning to think you'd gotten lost on your way up here," King Kronus called, and he came towards him with a smile. He clapped Thrayke on the shoulder and eyed his haul. "Collecting keepsakes were we?" the King teased, and he shrugged.

"Yeah, I couldn't help myself. How about you? I bet that movie collection didn't get left behind?"

"No chance, I spent years getting them together and absolutely wasn't about to leave them back on Earth," Kronus replied with his hand over his heart, as though offended at the sheer thought of leaving it behind, and Thrayke was glad he'd taken the bait to talk about something other than Thrayke's haul. He input his door code and grabbed the last of his cases, including the one with Kyra inside. As he stepped over the threshold into his quarters, he had to clench his jaw to stop from objecting when Kronus followed him in.

"I thought you'd be watching from the helm, sire?" he asked, and positioned his luggage in a corner as far away from his leader as possible. In the moment, he was eternally grateful that she was mute, but was worried she might panic and move inside the case, or worse, open it up to try and get some fresh air now that they'd come to a stop.

"I don't want to see it," Kronus answered, and his voice faltered a little. He then took a look around the office Thrayke had already had delivered to his private living quarters that consisted of an office, bunk, and private bathroom. He'd had his entire office from The Tower brought up to the mother ship shortly before in a conscious effort not to bring attention to the fact he hadn't intended on heading home with them, and was now glad he had. Thrayke felt oddly at home among his things, and watched Kronus through his carefully calm guise. "Do you think she's suffering? I couldn't bring myself to check on her, but I know you kept a close eye. How was she?"

Thrayke sighed, and his gaze instinctively fell back on the case he knew Kyra was listening from. As much as he didn't want to doubt her feelings for him, he couldn't forget how easily Kronus had stolen her away before. Thrayke knew he'd preyed on her pain and loathing of Kronus and his selfish nature to ensure she remembered who was there for her when he had discarded her so easily, and couldn't bear it if she eventually chose Kronus over him. Thrayke had proven his worthiness as keeper of her heart ten times over, but still fretted that he might still lose again so easily.

"The burden she carried killed her months ago, my King. She won't suffer," he answered, and watched as Kronus swallowed the lump in his throat.

"As much as it pains me to believe, perhaps it's true. Maybe she'll be better off this way. I made a lot of mistakes where she was concerned, and I've no doubt I'll make them all over again when I'm Mariah's husband," he replied, with a dry laugh. "She'll hate me, of course, but no more than I hate myself. The mission was a success, but other than that, we're returning home nothing more than empty shells of our former selves, Thrayke. I'm not a King, not anymore. I'm a spoiled, selfish Prince, and you are to call me as such from now on. You did more as a leader than I ever did, and I'm going to make you a Chief when we get home."

Thrayke was dumfounded. He didn't know what to say or how to respond, and practically fell into his seat at the huge desk he'd sat behind for decades. He'd always wanted recognition for his hard and honorable work to the crown, but hadn't worked hard all those years with only his desires as his goal. It was a dream come true to be made a Chief, of course, but he'd served Kronus willingly and out of respect, never for his own agenda. He was also acutely aware of how he'd lied to, and was continuing to lie to, his leader about the woman they both loved. Kronus had come to him for closure, and instead he was leaving with nothing but more lies, when he'd just offered his old friend a title of incredible worth and standing within the Thrakorian government back home. Traditionally, each King had only one Chief, but many of Kronus's siblings had appointed numerous ones, and he had seemingly decided to follow their example.

"It's been an honor serving you over the years, Prince Kronus. I don't need titles or recognition to continue doing so, just a place at your side and a promise of more adventures to come, but I will accept whatever designation you wish to give me. I did so the day you named me the Besieger, and will do so again," Thrayke replied, and stood to embrace his friend.

"Very well then," Kronus said, and he then left Thrayke's quarters without another word.

***

When the case was finally opened, it took Kyra a few seconds to get her bearings. Her eyes eventually focused in the dim light, and she saw what appeared to be Thrayke's exact office from The Tower, but simply plucked from Earth and deposited aboard the huge ship. He was standing over her, his hand outstretched for her to take, and she took it. Kyra's legs wobbled slightly and ached after being curled up for so long, but her strong man put an arm around her waist and kept her upright, and she smiled.

"The doors are locked tight, so no one's getting in without a blowtorch," he told her, and settled his lover in a perched position against the desk. Kyra nodded in understanding and then accepted a glass of water from him, which she promptly downed. She was parched, and the cool liquid was a more than welcome relief to her dry throat.

It was a few seconds before she had a proper look around, and Kyra immediately spied the window to one side of the huge room. Right now, it was frosted over, and she touched it expecting it to be bumpy, but instead it was smooth. Thrayke then pressed a button on a large panel to the right, and it went translucent instantly.

Kyra's mouth dropped open. From the huge window she could see out into the vastness of space as it stretched out all around them, but what held her gaze wasn't the abundance of stars or the brightness she hadn't considered could be present up there—it was the planet dominating the space before her. Earth seemed so near she felt she could reach out and touch it, but she also knew it was thousands of miles away, despite the deceiving sight.

Why did you bring me here? You said you were planning to stay behind in the end? she signed.

"Because all was not as I'd once thought, and the only way we could be safe was to sneak you here with me," Thrayke replied, and he stepped close to her from behind. He pressed a kiss on her shoulder and snaked his arms around her waist, staring down at the planet below from over her shoulder. "I only found out early this morning that it wasn't safe to stay behind like I'd planned, and knew I had to come and get you."

What's the show? she asked again, and Thrayke sighed.

"The name many of our kind have given to today, and what's about to happen. Fifty years ago we began preparing for our invasion, and it seems measures were put in place to ensure we had adequate time in which to complete our mission. Your planet was a mess. Earth was overpopulated and its eco-system and natural resources had been overused to the point of extinction."

She nodded, still peering down at the planet she couldn't deny had been abused by its indigenous inhabitants for far too long. "Earth was dying, Kyra. There was seismic activity all across the globe, and we had to put measures in place to stop them. Holes were drilled into the Earth's core, and special casings were sent down into them right before we came on Invasion Day. The substance within surrounded the magma, causing chaos within the planet's mantle. It then stabilized it and held it in controlled stasis, but came at a great cost. We had to use an incredibly valuable metal to Thrakor called Coranium to put a stopper in your planet's cataclysm. Because of our withdrawal, Kronus recently issued an order instructing that the Coranium be retrieved once all the DNA positive humans were safely aboard this ship, and that's why you felt the ground shaking in Los Angeles. That city will be one of the first to crumble as it sits on one of the most dangerous of Earth's fault lines, and when I discovered the truth, part of me wondered if I might already be too late to save you."

Kyra looked back over her shoulder at him, and took in the weary, hard-worn frown that dominated Thrayke's face. He still looked his usual self, but he wore his pain openly, and she frowned.

I'm sorry for what I thought I wanted. Up on that rooftop, I realized I didn't want to die, but it was almost too late. When you pulled me back, it was such a relief, and I know now I can't be selfish anymore. If you really want me, I'm yours. Now, forever, always... she signed.

"Forsaking all others?" he asked, and she turned to properly look into his eyes as she gave him the answer he seemed to need so desperately.

Forsaking all others. You are mine and I am yours, for life.

When they could finally tear themselves away from each other, Kyra took a shower and was pleased to find some combats that fit waiting for her with Thrayke's luggage. She was too short to pass for a Thrakorian, but guessed that at least she wouldn't stand out too much in the black combats everyone wore if she was ever forced to leave his quarters, rather than in her civilian clothes.

Kyra looked out the window again, and part of

her wished she hadn't. Earth was already ablaze with fiery magma, and her heart bled for all the lives that had to have already been lost to its flow.

"They don't deserve to die, but we were never there to save everyone, only those that mattered—despite how awful that sounds. The Gentry and the highest-regarded humans are aboard, and have been put into stasis along with the DNA profiled candidates ready to work for us on Thrakor. Technically, you can join them, but I don't think Kronus would take too kindly to discovering how we sneaked you aboard. For now, you need to stay hidden, and safe. We'll figure everything out later, okay?"

Okay, she agreed, still watching the show with a frown. *Why are we staying to watch?*

"In case there are any stragglers. Only once it's all over and we know for sure that none of our comrades will be left behind can we leave. Our race is proud of our laws and our ability to follow orders. King Thrakor is a ruler, but also a warrior. He took our people and gave them purpose and structure, just like we did for you. Perhaps we aren't so different, after all," he said with a small laugh, and then checked his tablet device to see if there were any updates with regards to the itinerary. "We should be leaving in a few hours," he informed her, and Kyra paled. It suddenly dawned on her, if they were waiting for stragglers, that could mean only one thing, and it hurt to even contemplate.

You won't leave until the Earth is dead, along with everything on it, will you?

"No," was all he could seem to answer. Thrayke reached out to offer her a supportive touch, but she yanked her arm away. Nothing a Thrak could offer her would bring her comfort right now, regardless of her love for him. She needed a minute, and was grateful when he seemed to understand that need without having to question her.

Kyra then watched the world that was her home perish. She couldn't tear her eyes away, and felt she owed it to those dying at the hands of their angry planet to stay watch and morn them. She sat curled in a ball on the floor, and watched as the many spots of evidently gushing lava turned from red to black, along with some of the once blue oceans and white ice caps. The end of the world was happening right before her eyes, and there was nothing she could do about it. She thought it was finally over when all stilled, and she almost turned back to look at Thrayke, when she saw something start to move again.

Tears streamed down her face, and soundless screams roared from her lungs as her home planet imploded. Piece by piece it crumbled in on itself, evidently caving in to fill the voids left behind from the once spewing magma. Kyra pounded her fists against the window with rage, and screamed curses out into the heavens as the planet crumbled and perished. When all that was left of planet Earth splintered into huge pieces and then disintegrated into shards destined to float among the debris of space, she doubled over and wailed.

It was only when Thrayke pinned her to him and put his hand over her mouth that she realized she was screaming for real, and hearing her voice again after so long was suddenly so alien to her that Kyra immediately quieted.

Was that me? she signed when she was calmer, even though she knew it had to have been.

"Yes, I don't know how, but you've managed to dislodge something, or perhaps you simply got it to heal by sheer force. Take it easy, you sounded a bit croaky," he told her, and she nodded.

Sobs were still catching in her throat, and when

she looked back at the emptiness of space behind, Kyra had to turn away again. She couldn't bring herself to consider the carnage the human race had just brought on its own world because of its historic foolhardiness, but also the destruction the Thrakorian's had let happen once they no longer needed what Earth had to offer.

The feelings of despair for the loss of human life weren't her burden to bear, she knew, but she still felt lost, and Kyra pressed herself into Thrayke's strong hold. He wrapped himself around her tightly, and didn't let go until she let him.

"I love you," she whispered, and the sound of her still croaky voice made her wince, but it was a wondrous sound, and one she was still shocked to have back after having spent so long in silence.

"I love you, too," he replied. "I'm going to make all of this better, believe me…"

She did, and knew that while everything she'd once known had been lost, the most important piece of her heart was right beside her, keeping her safe. All they had to do now was survive the chaos both knew had to be coming their way.

***

The end of book two in the Invasion Day series

ABOUT THE AUTHOR

LC Morgans is an author with an obsession for telling powerful stories. Not a day goes by that she doesn't immerse herself in other worlds, and her desire to write about them came from an early age. Shutting off her imagination was never an option, so the stories came to life inside her mind, and in time they'll all make it to the page.

She loves hearing from her fans and you can connect with her via the following:

www.facebook.com/LCMorgansauthor

If you enjoyed this book, please consider sharing your thoughts by leaving a review where you purchased this novel to help promote LC Morgans' work.

~~~~~~~~

Other novels by LC Morgans –

Humankind: Book 1 in the Invasion Day series

Made in the USA
Charleston, SC
27 August 2016